Elise's father wants her to marry Derrick . . . but who does her heavenly Father want her to marry?

"You will never be happy with a man as domineering as Derrick Homes," Trevor said. "How can you even think to do this?" He looked at her steadily.

"What kind of a man could I be happy with, Trevor?" Her dark eyes met his unflinchingly.

"With a man who understands your need to serve the Lord. With a man who has loved you all his life."

She drew in breath. Her head felt light. "I must honor my father. My promise ... "

"If you keep this promise, there will be no turning back for you. You will be rich and important, but you will never know true love." He turned away from her and clomped down the stairs two at a time, slamming the front door behind him.

With uncertainty in her step, Elise went back to her father's room to pray with him and prepare herself for a wedding.

SHIRLEY S. ROHDE, an author of many short stories and articles, debuts with her first inspirational romance novel, *Sisters in the Sun*. Shirley lives in Pennsylvania where she and her husband enjoy woodcrafting and being grandparents.

Sisters in the Sun

Shirley S. Rohde

Heartsong Presents

<u>*Dedication*</u>
To my wonderful husband, Norman
and our great family,
and especially, Elsie.
And to the memory of my mother.

A note from the Author:
I love to hear from my readers! You may write to me at the following address:

Shirley S. Rohde
Author Relations
P.O. Box 719
Uhrichsville, OH 44683

ISBN 1-55748-672-7

SISTERS IN THE SUN

one

The train clacked along, speeding Elise home at an almost alarming rate. Over and over, she heard the wheels sing on the lightning rails, "Home for good, home for good!"

Elise remembered the exact moment when her father had told her and Nettie that they were to be sent to separate boarding schools. The memory gave her a cold sensation at the back of her neck that even her heavy coil of dark hair couldn't dispel. She had been nine and Nettie barely seven. Their father's announcement had shattered their world.

The early morning mist had hung over the little valley below their family home. Everything had seemed shrouded by the mist, she remembered, as though her life had gone into mourning. She remembered the promise she had made to Nettie after their mother died, to look after her always, and Elise's eyes darkened and her teeth chewed at her full lips.

She wondered how Nettie had changed. Would they be able to pick up the lost years? They hadn't been able to share many holidays, and the distance between them had grown wider year by year, as though Nettie had made her adjustments and had gone on with her life.

Elise's nervous fingers clutched at the folds of her dark suit. She couldn't deny that she had enjoyed some parts of boarding school, the learning and the camaraderie with the other girls, but she had missed Nettie.

For a time, letters had come with regularity from Nettie, though seldom from their father. But after a time, the letters' arrival became sporadic, then stopped all together, and Elise had become an island to herself, waiting for today, the day she would be done with boarding school forever.

Now that this day had come at last, she felt as though the mist from her home's valley was claiming her once again, clouding her happiness, casting shadows over her future and the relationships that were once so dear. She shivered in the warm car.

In the other seat a young matron commented to Elise on the weather, and Elise wrenched her attention away from her thoughts. She faltered into conversation about the sooty ride, then feigned a weak smile and broke off mid-sentence. The woman resumed her reading. Elise stared absently at the magazine's cover, noticing the date: May 1906.

Her breath caught. Had it really been seven years since her mother had fallen to her death on the cliffs behind the Traum? Elise shook her head in disbelief, then self-consciously checked to see if her companion's eyes were still on her magazine. The woman appeared absorbed by her reading, and Elise's thoughts claimed her once more.

The Traum, the sprawling mansion that was her home, had been named by her father. The Traumerei, he had once called it, a word that meant "dream." Built high on the bluff overlooking the small town of Schiffley, the house was the fulfillment of his dreams, the culmination of his hard work and the epitome of the love he had found with Edwynna. The townspeople soon shortened the name to Traum, and now even Wilhelm had accepted it.

Again the other woman in the car interrupted Elise's

thoughts, her honeyed voice breaking through Elise's rev-
erie. "I am going home to see my family. My husband can't
often get away, his business commitments, you know. Do
you travel much?" Her question had a breathless quality
and there was anticipation in her face as she waited for
Elise to speak.

"I'm. . .I'm going home from school. I'm meeting my
father and then my sister's train." Elise closed her lips,
offering no more than she had been asked. Reluctantly, the
woman paged through the magazine again.

Elise breathed a small sigh of relief, and her thoughts
drifted to Trevor. A soft smile crept to her lips. They had
been children together in the large kitchen at the mansion.
In her mind's eye, she could almost see those long-ago
children. Flour had covered their faces as they helped Cook
make cakes for Elise's mother to give to the orphan children. Remembering, Elise's hand flew to her cheek, as
though brushing away powdery residue. She had been seven
and Trevor fourteen. Nettie tired easily of rolling and stamp-
ing out the biscuits, but Elise and Trevor had been a team,
filling the trays with shortbread cutouts and stacking the
baked ones. The cookies' crisp brown edges had tempted
them as they worked.

She wondered if Trevor had completed his education to
become a doctor. Her own mother had been his benefactor,
offering to pay his tuition so he could help his people to a
better life. Elise prayed that her father had honored that
commitment.

Elise had never thought much about the fact that Trevor
was her Nanny's brother, but she understood now that for
a boy who had to come to the Traum for day-old bread to
help feed his large family, becoming a doctor was no easy

feat. His keen mind had been brimming with curiosity, though, and his young face had always seemed full of the goodness of Christian love. As Elise anticipated meeting him after their long separation, she felt a tingle run along her nerves.

Once again, however, her fellow traveler attempted to engage her in conversation, and finally Elise gave in to it, skirting the subject of the meeting with her father.

"You will have to come and visit me if you should ever be in Philadelphia again. Here's my husband's card," the woman said, her voice filled with her own importance. "Did you say your father is a businessman? Perhaps he knows my Frank."

Elise studied the card and thanked the woman, knowing she would never honor the invitation. "Probably not," she answered demurely. "My father has a small business in Schiffley, you may have never even heard of it."

The woman's pale eyes raised questioningly. Elise nodded and permitted herself to drift in dull conversation. She was relieved when the conductor came through the car and announced the stop for Baumanstown.

"I wonder why we're stopping here," the woman complained. "These locals have all kinds of monotonous delays. Milk stops, Frank calls them." She colored sightly as Elise stood up and began lowering her valises from the baggage rack.

"My stop," Elise answered lightly. The pounding in her heart seemed to blot out the woman's reply. For a second, Elise swayed in the aisle as she prayed, "I can do all things through Christ which strengthens me." She gave her companion a hasty nod, and then Elise stepped gingerly up the aisle as the train pulled into the small depot.

The world was changing much too fast.

On one hand Wilhelm liked the prospect of change. At fifty-two, he still had dreams of making Schiffley a major city. Now that immigration was slowing, the town's expansion was becoming solid middle class. Business was flourishing; the community bustled with activity and progress. He preferred not to think of the "old town" with its dilapidated houses and factories and the people he termed riffraff.

On the other hand, he didn't like all the trappings that came with progress. The very ingredients that would bring prosperity to his world were not completely desirable, and he would be the first to resist them.

He didn't like the automobiles that were going twenty miles an hour, passing sedate buggies, scaring horses, and putting foolish notions in young men's heads until they dressed like rakes and acted like fools. He didn't like the noises the horseless carriages made, nor the smells of the engines in the fresh countryside, nor the way they dug ruts into fine carriage roads and desecrated the landscape, demanding right-of-way and wider bridges.

Just thinking of it brought him to an abrupt halt on the first rise he came to. The horses' ears twitched with the unexpected stop. Wilhelm sat gazing at the panorama stretching before him. A barn and farmhouse nestled into the land as though they belonged there.

He remembered vividly his humble beginnings in America, even though his first sight of this good land was now more than twenty-five years ago. He had never quite overcome his feeling of anguish over the hardships he had endured entering the country during the great depression of 1880. The disabling effects of that dismal time crippled American families as well as many young immigrants like himself. Recovery was long and slow and many chose to return to the Old World where they at least recognized their enemies, rather than stay and fight new ways.

Wilhelm, however, never gave up believing that the American dream was within his grasp. His dream simply waited and, after all the years when most men would have thought they had already attained their goal, Wilhelm's dream still persisted. It had been long detained and recharted. Only this time it was his children who would make the dream come true. They were the ones who would expand his small empire and bring new life to his silk mill and his town. He had come to an impasse, wanting a broader scope for himself and Schiffley. Through his daughters, though, he had at last found a way.

Gingerly, he drove the team back to the road. He had chosen the runabout for the trip because he liked the way the carriage handled with his prized team of horses. He also liked the stylish lamps on either side of the carriage. Annette, he knew, would be impressed, even if Elise was not.

The horses balked suddenly. They tried to jerk the carriage over a rut in the road, then stopped dead. Wilhelm jumped down to look at the damage. He slapped his hat across his hand in exasperation. The wheel had been snapped, broken beyond repair. He gritted his teeth and took off his coat, carefully laying it across one of the seats. Then he rolled up his sleeves and went to work unhitching the horses, all the while talking calmly to them in spite of his agitation. When the team was free, he rolled down his sleeves, put on his coat, straightened his hat, and led the horses downhill to the nearest farm.

As he walked, the sounds of the hooves became a rhythmic sound in his ears that seemed to repeat over and over, "Late for the train, late for the train." He was nearly drenched with perspiration when they reached the farmhouse. Nevertheless, he presented himself at the door with dignity and aplomb.

A half hour later, the team was pulling the farmer's wagon. Wilhelm was once more on his way to the depot, when he heard a commotion behind him. The horses bolted, tossing their heads and rolling their eyes wildly. He struggled to remain on the rough seat as a loud honking automobile demanded to pass. The team dove toward the ditch as they were forced off the narrow lane. Wilhelm shook his fist; the driver waved and smiled as he whizzed by, and Wilhelm recognized the old farmer who had sold him his rig just moments before.

After permitting his team a short rest, Wilhelm led them back on the main road. The girls would have to wait for their ride, and their vehicle was not quite as handsome as he had intended. The thought of an apology or explanation never entered his mind, however.

&

The car lurched, and Elise gripped the handle to steady herself. She scanned the narrow platform as the train came to a grinding halt. Her father was not in sight. Slowly, she picked up her bags and waited as the conductor opened the heavy metal door and swung down to lower the step. A hiss of steam greeted her. Another passenger descended to the platform, and then the conductor held out his hand to assist Elise. If her foot faltered for a second, it went unnoticed under the hem of her blue wool suit.

Again her dark eyes searched the small platform. Resignation sloped her square shoulders and she moved quickly to stand with her back to the brick station building, prepared to wait the hour for her sister's arrival.

As the train departed, her eyes momentarily met those of the passenger who had shared her seat. Elise saw the look of surprise on the young woman's face. The platform was deserted.

Well, the woman was no more surprised than she, Elise admitted to herself. The late spring breeze was chilly and she tied her bonnet ribbons more firmly under her chin and fastened the collar button of her suit. In spite of the stiff wind, she preferred the outside to the dusty ticket office and the agent's small talk.

Elise fingered through her reticule, looking for something, anything to occupy her time. The thought of the books in the bottom of her large valise made her long to rifle through it. For the third time, she studied the small watch on the gold chain around her neck. Only a half hour had passed. She sighed.

If only Nettie were here, then they could use this time to catch up with their lives. Elise's stomach knotted as she tried to think why her father hadn't come. Perhaps he was waiting for Nettie's later train.

Then she saw him, walking tall and unhurried across the back corner of the depot. He was dressed in the same somber clothing she had seen him wear for all of her seventeen years. He had lost some of his look of bluster and arrogance, though. Could the years have changed them both, she wondered. She dared to hope that her father had found some new meaning to his life.

She wanted desperately for him to find Christ. He had

been an errant Christian when her mother lived, but when Edwynna died, he vowed never to believe in anything again. Elise ached for his denial and his pain, and she hated the way it had affected all their lives.

"Hello, Papa," she said when at last he stood looking down at her. His beard had strands of white interspersed with the jet black, and craggy lines etched his cheeks.

"You beat me, Elise." He took a large pocket watch from under his long vest, scrutinized it, and quickly snapped it shut again. "Twenty-seven and a half minutes until Annette's train."

Elise blinked. She hadn't seen her father for fourteen months, but he had no word of greeting for her, no question of her health, no notice of how she had grown and matured, that she was no longer a child but a young woman. Tears stung her eyes in spite of her resolve.

Wilhelm went inside the ticket office and there he remained until five minutes before Nettie's scheduled arrival.

In the interim, Elise admitted to herself that except for his increasing age, her father was not likely to have changed at all. She prayed for them all. She could only wonder what life at the Traum was like now and how her step-mother and stepbrother had fared.

When she and her father faced each other again, they both shifted their eyes awkwardly away from each other's faces, as though they were strangers. Several times both started to speak, only to fall into a heavy silence once more. When the whistle blew in the distance, together they turned in relief toward their only bond: Nettie's homecoming.

Three passengers descended from the huge iron train and hurried to their destinations. Nettie was not among them. The train roared away with the same bluster that had brought it.

Wilhelm said something under his breath and walked toward the back of the depot where the horses waited, hitched to the farmer's wagon. Elise picked up her bags and followed him. Once again, she repeated the prayer, though she said it aloud and with greater fervor this time. "I can do all things through Christ which strengthens me."

A chill wind stirred the loose hairs around her face, and gray clouds hid the sun. The weather, however, was no drearier than this homecoming had turned out to be.

two

Elise paced back and forth in the upstairs hall where she could watch the large circular driveway from the balcony windows. No word had come from Nettie. Elise had begged her father to return to the depot for the next train, but because it was not due for several hours, he refused, leaving Nettie to her own devices if she arrived to an empty platform.

Inger, Elise's stepmother, had been amused that Nettie had not come on time. She laughed and shook her head, crossing her hands on her round belly which was poorly concealed by her white apron. She insisted on wearing the apron every day, though she never lifted a finger in the kitchen unless it was to open a pot on the stove to give her approval of the food.

She gave Elise a great hug that seemed to last long after she let go. The two had become allies, uniting to keep their faith against the tirades of Wilhelm. Although they didn't always succeed in changing his ultimatums, they had joined in a strange friendship born of survival.

Inger's son Justin, on the other hand, had greeted Elise coolly. He had been keenly disappointed that Nettie was not with them. He argued loudly with his stepfather to at least send the carriage for her. When he started off to the depot himself, Wilhelm stopped him with a look. Justin then sulked off to his room.

Now Elise saw a movement on the road, and she pressed

her face to the pane. She watched in disbelief as a cream-colored automobile rounded the driveway at breakneck speed. The open seat in the rear was piled high with luggage and boxes that teetered precariously as the Packard came to a screeching halt. A female passenger, hunched down beside the driver, waved and sat straighter as the man quickly jumped out and ran around to open her door. A box tumbled off the seat and scattered its contents on the stone driveway. The woman craned her neck to see what had fallen.

Only then did Elise recognize her sister. She raced down the stairs, skipping the last two, screaming, "Nettie is home, Nettie is home!"

Upstairs a door opened and Justin appeared. The cook and a kitchen maid came to peer out behind the lace curtains.

Elise opened the front door and ran to the drive, ignoring the pouty look on Nettie's face as she stood surveying the damaged box and its contents. Elise clasped her in an embrace that almost toppled them both, and Elise laughed until she cried.

Nettie offered a cheek as Elise kissed her again. Finally, she stepped away and stood looking up at the house. "Did you ever think we'd be standing here again, Lise?" She wiped a few tears from her eyes, hugged Elise again, then hugged her arms around herself. "All those dreadful years when we had to kiss the hems of the teachers' dowdy dresses, this is where I wanted to be. You must know what I mean."

"It's so wonderful to see you again, Nettie. It's all behind us now. When you go back it won't be for very long—and then we'll both be home for good."

"How you've changed, Lise. You're a lady now. Does Papa know?" Nettie's voice was serious.

"I don't think so, Nettie. It doesn't matter. He will. And look at you, dear sister. You're as beautiful as Mamma ever was."

The driver, a young man in his twenties, had finished piling Nettie's bags on the porch and came now to stand beside her, gazing at her in adoration. She held out her hand and permitted him to kiss it before she dismissed him with a whisper. Reluctantly, he drove off, all the time looking wistfully back at Nettie.

Wilhelm arrived on the porch just in time to see the back of the Packard. Any questions he might have had regarding Nettie's mode of transportation died on his lips as his younger daughter turned to face him. He studied her from head to toe, from the length of the skirt that exposed most of her ankle, to the large strawberry-colored hat, perched slightly askance on her upswept hair, and downward again to the long, feathered boa that draped gracefully around her high-necked blouse. For an instant, he was stunned by her resemblance to her mother.

He was aghast, however, at Nettie's attire. He watched as Elise hugged her sister again, and mentally, he compared the two girls: their equal height, their straight delicate noses, their ruddy complexions. Nettie's waist was decidedly smaller, he noted, her hair a soft shimmering blond, drawn up from her dimpled face, while Elise's thick black hair was neatly coiled at the nape of her neck; Nettie's eyes were deep blue, and Elise's were dark like his own. Nettie's face held breathless anticipation, he thought, as though she were in a hurry to live the next five minutes, or fifteen, or all of life. Elise was more sedate, as though she had been tempered into a fine lady. Only her sparkling eyes transformed her face.

"Oh, how I've missed you, Nettie," she was saying. "Isn't she just beautiful, Papa, and so grown up?"

"She looks like a tart," Wilhelm said under his breath, but he took both Nettie's hands and looked deeply into her eyes, searching for some response known only to him. Not finding it, he kissed her cheek lightly and mumbled a greeting.

Justin could no longer stay in the background. He grabbed Nettie by the waist and swung her around until she squealed in protest. "Nettie, dear Nettie, how I have missed you." His face had suddenly become animated. "I would have come to pick you up myself had you asked me." He was breathless as he led her up the steps to Inger. There he jiggled impatiently as greetings were made and baggage carried away. "I couldn't wait until you came home. The house has been such a bore. We'll be saddled up and riding in no time. I hope you haven't forgotten how."

Nettie's laughter filled the hall, and the servants standing nearby smiled to each other. "Give me time to catch my breath, Justin." She gave him a sweeping curtsey.

"Very well, but I won't be put off for long, sis. How about tomorrow morning at seven?"

Justin had filled out from his former skinny youth, Elise noticed. He was handsome in a frail sort of way. When he lost his smile, though, his face wore a wary expression, and he still had the annoying habit of staring.

"You mean you won't permit me one morning to lie in bed and be thankful I am no longer at school?" She laughed when her father harumphed loudly.

Inger bustled around the girls and caught their hands

again. "Now good it is to have my *liebchens* home. To-night at supper your Papa has a surprise for you." She held a finger to her lips to keep the secret for the proper time. Her blue eyes twinkled almost as brightly as Nettie's.

❧

The table setting was more elaborate than any of them remembered. Candles graced each end; the soft light played across the silver and fine china. The centerpiece of flowers were removed from the table when the roast goose with all the trimmings was carried in.

"Pinch me, or are we having Christmas dinner?" Elise commented to no one in particular. There was an air of festivity that she had not felt at the depot. Even her father had a mischievous grin as be carved the bird.

"It was Inger's idea to make this a feast."

Inger flushed sightly. "Only to make the surprise more wonderful for our daughters," she said modestly.

"I can't keep it any longer, daughters." Wilhelm stopped carving, the knife poised in the air. "We are planning a party to celebrate your homecoming. It has been far too long since we've had any kind of party in this house." He puffed out his chest as he looked at the amazed expressions on both his daughters' faces. "It's still in the planning stages, but mark my word, it will be the biggest gala Schiffley has ever seen."

Nettie clapped her hands, then pulled Justin out of his chair and they danced around the table. "I love parties. I will have a new dress, of course," she laughed.

Wilhelm's disapproving look quickly sat them down again. "Both my daughters will have new dresses to show them off."

Inger nodded approvingly.

Elise got caught up in Nettie's enthusiasm. "What's the occasion, Papa?" She watched his face, wondering at his rare mood and confused about the celebration of their home-coming, since Nettie still had to return to school.

"I'm hoping it will be a special night just to celebrate together. We will discuss it more, later." He winked slyly at Elise.

She frowned, filled with the sudden premonition that something was amiss. Without leaving the table she began to pray, blotting out all else, as her mother had taught her to do years ago. The meal was quiet and unhurried, even festive, and her father was in the best of moods, but Elise had the distinct feeling something was wrong. Suddenly, her father was paying attention to her for the first time since her arrival; what was he thinking? As always when she had a sense of foreboding, she turned to God.

❧

Accustomed to the friendly closeness of dormitory life, the girls sought each other out more quickly than they had expected. Within minutes of retiring to their own bedrooms, their doors were opened, and the sisters were seated on Nettie's bed. The conversation was strained at first, but soon they were chattering as though they had never been separated.

The room hadn't been changed since they went away to school. The same toys were stacked tidily in one corner, and the same dolls and stuffed bears looked down from the shelf high above the dressers, as though awaiting the return of their young mistress.

Nettie's assorted wardrobe lay scattered around the room. She monopolized the conversation about friends and parties and the supervised dances with a nearby boys' school.

Elise soon began to realize her sister's interests were not the same as her own. She grew quiet.

Nettie asked, "Don't you ever think of boys, Elise?"

"Of course I do." Elise blushed, glad Nettle was primping in the mirror, pinching her cheeks to a rosy red and running her fingers over her lips until they colored.

"Some of the girls use lip rouge—in secret, of course. The head mistress wouldn't permit it. I even bought some on my last trip to town. You can use it if you'd like."

"Papa would have our hides," Elise laughed and felt more relaxed. "Consider the lilies of the field. Even Solomon was not arrayed like one of these. You are like a lily of the field, Nettie, more beautiful than you could ever be with all the rouge you could own."

"I can't believe you are still doing that, Lise, quoting from the Bible, just like Mamma taught us. How quaint!"

"Nettie!"

"Well, it is! No one goes around spouting off like that anymore."

To hide the hurt she felt, Elise jumped to her feet. "Let me brush your hair the way I used to when we were children."

Nettie quickly took the chair in front of the oval mirror and unfastened her upswept hair. Her pinched cheeks had returned to their normal rose-tinted pallor, and with the golden hair streaming down her back, she looked like an innocent child. Elise stood behind her and gasped at her sister's reflection; she looked almost exactly like a younger version of their mother. Elise's eyes stung with memory and tears.

"To blazes with lilies anyway. My teacher said it would be all right for a party." Nettie's eyes met Elise's in the mirror, but Elise let the remark slide.

"Papa is planning to show us off to all the eligible men, you know," Nettie observed as her hair was being brushed. "He doesn't fool me. It's the whole reason for the party. Think about it. Have you ever seen him look so happy?"

The brush paused. "How can you be so sure?" Elise sank to the bed.

"Because I know Papa. We haven't had a real party since Mamma died. I remember sneaking out on the balcony and looking down at Mamma and the fancy dresses that came to her parties. There was none like hers, though."

"You may be right about Papa," Elise reasoned, acknowledging the reason for her anxiety over the announcement. "I will be the first to go, you know, and I haven't had time to do anything with my life." Her voice was flat, and she laid back on the bed, staring at the ceiling. "You will be next, and then we'll be off Papa's hands for good."

Nettie wrinkled her nose. "Well, I for one am glad I'm not the oldest daughter. You know how European Papa is when it comes to doing things. It will give me time to figure a way out."

Elise sat up and stared at her sister. "Nettie, don't you care that I am about to be thrown to the wolves?"

"Of course I care, Lise. It makes it that much sooner for me." She was piling her hair on top of her head again. "Makes me look older, don't you think?"

"Yes, and I don't like it."

"Justin liked it. I saw it in his eyes."

"He's your brother, silly."

"My stepbrother. I think you're jealous of him, especially the way he and Papa get along now. I saw them talking and laughing together. It is about time. He has paid his debt for being a stepson. Justin likes to be praised, to feel important. Surely you can't blame him for that." Nettie was suddenly very serious.

"Since when did you get to be so wise when it comes to men?" Elise studied her sister more closely. Nettie had definitely changed.

"Some of the lessons I learned at school were not from the teachers. Most of it came from listening to the older girls. For one thing, I know you should be more tolerant of Justin. He's a very important member of this family."

"You didn't go to school to learn about boys, Nettie."

Nettie laughed. "Oh, no?"

"You're shameless." Elise had to laugh. "I'm not blaming Justin. I'd be willing to meet him halfway, but he completely ignores me, as though I'm not there."

"I think he's afraid of you," Nettie almost whispered. "He told me once he thought you were so perfect."

"What?" Elise gasped.

"Oh, pooh." Nettie shrugged her shoulders. "Justin doesn't mix well, that's all." She added carefully, "And sometimes you are a little overbearing."

Elise's eyes smarted. After a long moment she said, "I longed for you to come home, Nettie, and now that you have. . .things seem so different. I don't know. It's like we don't fit anymore. Not just me, but you, too."

"I'll make us fit." Nettie tossed a pillow at Elise. Elise laughed, then threw it back.

Nettie was the first to stop. "I have something to say to Papa that will change his happy mood."

"What could be that earth shattering?"

"This is bound to do it." Nettie stared out of the window to the fields far below the house. "I'm not going back to school." Elise recognized her sister's expression from when they were children; Nettie was determined to have her own way.

Elise tried to make light of the statement by saying, "Oh, yes, you will. I can tell you it just doesn't work with Papa if you say you're not going to do something. You just told me you learned something about men from the other girls, but I can give you a lesson on Papa. Mark my words. You'll go back to school." She thought of her own plight and how she would refuse to marry if Papa should expect it.

"I hate those old teachers and their strict rules," Nettie pouted.

"Nettie! You know they only have your best interest at heart. So does Papa really."

"I know that's what he says—but his best interest isn't always my best interest. Lise, we are young and Papa's such a prude. Women are working and doing lots of things. I want to be one of them."

"Maybe you just need to get away from school for awhile," Elise soothed, trying to hide her surprise.

"I'll run away before I go back to that dungeon, you'll see."

"Nettie, I really think you mean it." Elise put her hand on her sister's arm, feeling the tension under her soft skin.

"I can't be like you, always doing what's best for everyone else. I feel smothered. I want to know what the world is like outside of the Traum and school. Don't you? Don't you wonder what you're missing? We can't go to the local dances, or have men call for us, or anything the girls in town can do. There's more to life than doing tiresome tapestries and learning how to run a house. Why I bet Papa even has our husbands picked out."

Elise didn't want to think about that supposition. "But you had dances at school," she argued.

"They were attended by spoiled little rich boys—and the chaperons were straight-laced old maids and we could hardly even steal a kiss." She clapped her hands over her mouth and turned beat red.

"Nettie, you didn't!"

"Promise not to tell. I only tried it twice. Promise!" She put her hands around her sister's neck in a light grip.

"You know I won't tell. What's it like?" Elise asked solemnly, looking away as though she wasn't sure she wanted to hear the answer.

"Dry, like kissing a prune," Nettie giggled. "But I liked it, no kidding, Lise. The head mistress used to try to make me fit into a mold. She would march around the room waving her finger at me." She raised her voice an octave higher and mimicked, "You must be more like your sisters in the society." She returned to a dull tone, "Did she ever care that it was killing me to be like everybody else?"

"Don't tell Papa about school until after the party," Elise begged. "I want time to think of my own life, too." There was the same look of determination on her face that had been on Nettie's.

"Do you have any plans?"

"I want to help the people in town. . .they're so poor."

"I knew it would be something noble," Nettie moaned.

Elise ignored her. "And when the right man comes along I want to be swept off my feet the way Mamma was swept off hers—though I have a hard time believing it was Papa doing the sweeping."

"That's a lot of wishes. I hope you get at least one of

them granted—and that it will be the swept-off-your-feet wish, like in the fairy stories. The other wish is lonely."

"You did learn something about life. I hope you find what you are looking for, too, Nettie."

"Promise not to tell Papa, Lise."

Elise placed her hands on Nettie's shoulders and reminded her, "We share secrets but we don't tell them." She smiled, glad for the opportunity to keep their secrets. "Do you know what Papa sees when he looks at you, Nettie?"

Nettie shook her head.

"He sees Mamma. I saw him staring at you all through dinner. It was as though no one else was in the room. Maybe getting what you want won't be as difficult as you imagine."

"It could be twice as hard. He could look at me and think, Edwynna would never do this." She grimaced and walked to her closet. "One thing more, Elise." She picked out a pair of new riding breeches and tossed them to her sister. "I want you to be ready to go riding at seven tomorrow. You will find out what a fine brother we have."

Elise left the room, breeches in hand, her sister still standing by the oval mirror. Elise had the skin-prickling sensation that Nettie considered herself the embodiment of their mother. Nettie, the peacemaker, the healer, the shining light. She wondered how this new role would affect life in the Traum. Life was definitely not going to be dull in the weeks ahead.

three

At precisely seven o'clock the horses were saddled and waiting in the driveway just outside the stable. The girls hurried up to them, leaving Justin behind.

"I want the big chestnut, Lise." Nettie ran over and gave the horse the carrot she had taken from the pantry. She giggled with delight. "The way Papa goes on about him you'd think he was the only horse in the stable." She stood back, admiring his rich color and fine lines. "You certainly are a beauty, Destry. I can see why he is so mad about you." The horse stamped impatiently. "Spirited, too. I like that."

Nettie's brown riding costume complemented her gracefully upswept hair and the small veiled derby perched to the side of her head. She fidgeted until she was helped to the saddle.

Justin grunted as he helped Elise onto the small mare, making no pretense at disguising his displeasure at having a third party on their outing. His riding coat creased softly with a comfortable worn look that Nettie's hadn't yet achieved. Turning to Nettie, he said loudly, "Next time you decide to ask anyone to come along, you had better consult me first."

Elise shot a meaningful glance at Nettie as she led the way across the field to the riding trail. She wore the new breeches Nettie had given her, but the remainder of her costume consisted of a boyish-looking jacket and a wide-brimmed sun hat tied loosely under her chin.

As the mare picked up speed, the hat flew rakishly behind Elise's long loose hair. She gave the mare her head and they cantered off well ahead of Nettie and Justin.

"Now you've gone and offended her," Nettie complained. "Really, Justin," she scolded as she led the horse daintily to the path. "I tried so hard to bring you two together. I want you to be friends, the way we are. Don't you think you could be more congenial? Lise is willing to give it a fair try if you will."

Her horse jerked impatiently. Justin caught the reins and held him. He leaned far out of his saddle and kissed Nettie lightly on the cheek. "I wanted you all to myself this morning, sis. It's been a long time since we talked. By the way, did I tell you how fetching you are in your riding habit?" He grinned as he let the reins drop and began to pick up the pace.

"Thank you, Justin. Let's hurry. I'm sure Elise will be at the farm before we are." Without waiting, she pulled ahead of him. Eager to be off, Destry stretched out into a smooth gallop. Nettie's laughter could be heard through the misty valley.

The fog seemed to swallow her as she disappeared into the mist that hung over the path. By the time Justin caught up with her, they were both wet with dew, for the sun was only beginning to break through to the gentle hills and corn fields. Nettie slackened Destry's pace to an easy gait. Justin sulked as he rode behind.

"What can I do to make up for taking advantage of a gorgeous day and the feel of a wonderful horse? Forgive me, Jus. I felt so free again."

A smirk crossed his face as he dug his heels into his

horse's flanks and raced ahead of her.

"Brat," she called after him. In a few minutes she was on his trail, proving that Destry was a capable horse. "You tricked me," she laughed as she matched his speed. He rode even faster. Breathlessly, she conceded. "You win, you win."

Finally, she came to a halt on the hill above the little valley where the farm spread out before them. The buildings were long and low, unlike the local farms with their two-story barns. Two of the buildings accommodated livestock and a third was headquarters to the workers on the farm. Justin came alongside Nettie and helped her down. They stood looking at the scene below them before they mounted again and began the long descent to the bottom of the valley.

≈

When Elise came upon the valley, the sight that greeted her was one so satisfying that her joy became a spiritual experience, lifting her up to God's heart. She had always loved this valley, even more than the Traum.

Familiar sights and sounds filled her senses as she began her descent down the well-worn road. The little mare was unhurried, as though reveling in her own good fortune. The fertile fields and tree-rimmed clearings enveloped horse and rider. Lazy slopes, bounded by rugged corrals with horses grazing in the pasture, embraced Elise with a feeling of peace.

Elise dismounted and began feeding some of the horses in the corral with apples from the sack on her saddle. On the other side of the pasture, in a separate enclosure, a white-faced chestnut whinnied. "We'll see if she likes apples, too," Elise said half aloud. She was about to open the gate when a hand on hers detained her. She stood still, looking up into the darkest eyes she had ever seen, a stranger, though with something familiar about his face.

"It's easier to ride to the other side than to walk across the field. Besides, you'll get your boots wet. This mare is in foal now. Your Papa wants to keep her segregated." He stared down into her eyes and their gazes held for a moment.

"Could it be Trevor?" She studied his sandy hair and returned to his compelling eyes.

He extended his hand. "One and the same, Miss Waller."

"When have we become so formal, Trevor?" She felt herself blush under his quick appraisal.

"When you became a woman, and I, your lowly servant." His unsmiling eyes never left her face.

"Trevor, we grew up together. Besides, I would never think of you or anyone else as a lowly servant." She spoke softly. Her damp hair curled against her face, and she pushed it away impatiently.

"People change, Miss Waller." He never looked away from her eyes, eyes nearly as dark as his. "I have something to show you that you may be interested in." He took her arm and together they walked into the first building.

The smell of fresh hay filled her nostrils. The building was dark and quiet except for the occasional neighing of a horse. At the last stall they stopped and he waited as she peered into the semi-darkness. "Why it's Prince." She held her cheeks and looked at him in confusion. "But I thought he was dead. Inger wrote that Prince had thrown Papa, and Papa had ordered him to be shot. I don't understand." Memory flooded her mind. Ever since she had been a child, Prince had been her favorite horse.

"He still remembers you, Elise." Her name slipped from Trevor's tongue as if by accident.

She reached above the chain and petted Prince as he rubbed his nuzzle against her shoulder. She looked up into Trevor's eyes again. His tone was softer now, and she realized he had spoken her name as easily as when they had been children. She was relieved.

"Your father was angry that night. There was a lightning storm and Prince got spooked; you know how he always hated thunder. Your father had to go on crutches for weeks—but later he was glad Prince hadn't been shot after all. We didn't tell your father until later, after his leg had mended. I was the stable boy that night, so it would have been my job to put Prince down. I couldn't do it. We fired the gun into the air and hoped for the best. We really thought it was over for us when your father found out, but it wasn't. He was glad. The horse does have a weakness in his hind leg from the fall, but he's still a good sire."

"It's been a long time, Trevor. Whatever would we have done without you as a friend? Saving horses and people." As they walked out into the daylight, she studied him again. His dark eyes were brooding, sometimes hinting at a smile, and his cheeks creased near his eyes in a way they never had when he was a boy. He had changed in a way that had made him more serious, more intense. "Thank you, Trevor." She held out her hand to him and felt the strength in his grasp. When she took her hand away, their fingers parted slowly, almost reluctantly.

"Have you begun your practice yet?" Something in his manner made it unnecessary to ask if he had finished school. His smile still froze her heart, and a small pulse quickened at her temple.

"No, but I'm working on it, and putting in some time here, too." He laughed. "Not much longer, I hope. It's good to see you again, Elise. I have a feeling you're not that same little girl I tried to convince to go away to school. Have you ever regretted it?"

"For awhile." She remembered back to that traumatic time. "It took a long time to get over being homesick."

At that moment Nettie and Justin came riding up the lane and sunlight flooded around them. Nettie seemed to poise in its warmth before she urged her horse along into the shadow.

"Edwynna," Trevor murmured in a barely audible whisper.

Elise heard and gasped, "It's Nettie."

Nettie got down, assisted by Trevor who took her slim waist in his two hands. "Can it be Trevor?" She embraced him. "I would have known you anywhere. You've grown so tall and you changed so little, more handsome perhaps." She smiled as though she enjoyed watching him color.

"Nettie." He shook her hand vigorously, the admiration in his eyes, undisguised.

Justin dismounted and brought tension to the reunion. He extended his hand. "It's a long time since we've seen you, old man. I rarely come to the lower stables. What's an old sawbones like you doing in a place like this?" The sarcasm never left his voice.

"I offered to do my brother's chores while he's down with the grippe. I won't have my own practice for a few weeks. I'm fixing up the old Driscol place for an office—with the help of many of my friends, of course."

"Still depending on everyone else for a handout," Justin observed.

"Never mind, Trevor. Justin may be only too glad for your advice someday," Elise defended.

Nettie began steering Justin toward the corral.

"On second thought," Justin pulled away abruptly, "see to it that my horse gets fed and watered before we take to the trails, old man."

Nettie quickly grabbed his arm. "You know it's bad for the horses to be overfed and watered before a ride. Justin, you're insufferable." She put the reins in his hand.

When they had gone, Elise said quietly, "Nettie can't help if she looks like our mother, Trevor."

For a moment his eyes clouded. "Just for a moment it was like ... "

"She's been having that effect on everyone."

"Too bad your mother died so young. She will be missed for a long, long time."

Elise was silent with her own thoughts. "I'm glad she is well-remembered," she said at last.

Trevor nodded. "Your father is another matter. All my family works for him. He controls everyone's lives with his low wages and poor working conditions. He keeps promising it will all change when the railroad comes to Schiffley. I can tell you this—the people can't live on promises. But the lord of the manor says soon, he can count the days. What do rich men know of living on empty promises, living with hunger? Those are the kind of days we count." He spoke through clenched teeth.

Elise's cheeks flushed hotly. "How dare you blame everything wrong in your life on my father? At one time he was as poor as even the poorest. He gives much to the town."

"Maybe when your mother lived he did. Not now."

"Perhaps if I talked to him he would make some changes. What if the railroad never comes?"

"Oh, it will come. I can guarantee it, Miss Waller, because you like the comfortable life and you do everything your father says. Well, don't disappoint all the people who are waiting on his promises."

He walked toward the paddock and let a young horse into the section where lush green grass covered the hillside. For a moment he stood there, leaning against the gate, his shirt rippling across his back in the stiff breeze. Then, without looking back, he walked up the path to the house.

Elise stared after him, pondering his words and their meaning. She rode away aimlessly, finally turning the mare toward the Traum. If Trevor was right about her father, than he was unfair to control the lives of so many. She prayed he was not so.

The birds in the treetops chirped with a lightness she did not share. To the east, dark clouds massed ominously over distant fields, and she marveled over the abrupt change in the weather. Even then, she didn't hurry the mare, for she needed time to think and pray before she spoke with anyone.

Approaching the upper stable, she heard voices raised in anger. Above the male voices, a girl pleaded for an end to the argument. Elise hurried to the large door.

Trevor was gesturing wildly, his face dark with rage. "These poor creatures are a disgrace." He pointed to the lathered, wheezing horses that stood behind Justin.

"We took them out to ride, not simply to look at," Justin retaliated.

"I'm to blame, Trevor," Nettie said sweetly. "We only thought to ride slowly and then we raced. We had so much fun." She laughed, then stopped, aware of the hollow sound in the rafters. Destry puffed his flanks and snorted. "Don't be mad at us, Trevor."

From the sidelines, Elise recognized Nettie's childlike tactics to get herself out of a difficulty. Her ploy seemed to work, for a little of the anger faded from Trevor's face.

"They're only horses, old man." Justin held onto his air of superiority. "That's why we hire the likes of you to clean them up." He pushed his crop at Trevor, who backed out of reach.

Elise's horse whinnied, and they turned to stare at her intrusion.

"Eavesdropping was always one of your habits, Elise," Justin accused. "I had hoped they might teach you some better manners at that fancy school that Papa spent so much money on."

Elise blushed and bit her lips. "There's no excuse for mistreating animals, Justin. Nettie, I expected better of you."

Nettie winked at Elise as she walked past her. "We meant no harm, Lise. This whole incident has gotten out of hand." At the same moment she shook her hair down from under the derby, and the gold that cascaded down her back was like a ray of sunlight let unexpectedly into the dark stable as the heavy clouds thundered outside. Elise watched as the men witnessed the vision with parted lips. The argument was over.

"Come with us, Lise. We're having lunch on the veranda if the rain doesn't spoil it." Since Nettie's return from school, Elise noticed she had taken to calling their porches verandas.

"Later, Nettie. I'll be up later."

After Nettie and Justin left, Elise brushed the mare and fed and watered her. She worked silently to care for the saddle on the post. Her head was pounding. At times she felt sick and dizzy. She was acutely aware of Trevor on the other side of the stable.

At long last he commented, "At least you had the decency to cool your mount down before you brought her in."

"She wasn't overheated," she answered tartly. "I wasn't with Nettie and Justin."

"Oh?" He worked steadily on Destry, covering him with a blanket now that the horse's wheezing had stopped. "Look at those ears, flopping all over the place. This horse is played out."

Elise wanted to run to the house and the quiet of her room. She closed her eyes for a few seconds to blot out the throbbing pain and hide the fact she was so close to tears. She forced herself to check the mare's legs, feeling the fronts and backs of each leg for splints and sprains. Satisfied, she took her saddle from the post and put it in the tack room.

Trevor met her halfway to the door, blocking her path. "I learned something today."

She hated to ask, but she did anyway. "What?"

"I learned that you girls are nothing like your ma. Nettie looks like her, but she's a poor imitation. You'd like to follow in her footsteps but not in a million years. Edwynna was a saint."

Tears welled in her eyes and she sank back against the rough pine boards. "My mother wasn't a saint nor would she have ever wanted to be called one. She was a good and caring woman with her own problems and shortcomings, just like anyone else. Papa used to say you had tender feelings for Mamma, and I think now he was right. In your own childish way, you were in love with her. But you're not a child anymore. If you're still obsessed with my mother, then I feel sorry for your patients."

"Now, why is that?" he breathed, close to her face.

"Because apparently, her death robbed you of your ability to show compassion. You have become hard and bitter. Mamma's sainthood increases with time. You put her on a pedestal so high you wouldn't even recognize the real woman anymore. She would have been very disappointed in the way life has changed you. I am disappointed, too, Trevor."

He flinched as though she had slapped him.

Elise leisurely brushed her breeches and squared her shoulders before she stood and matched his stare. Then she turned and walked briskly into the pouring rain, her head throbbing with each deliberate step.

She remembered how kind he had been to her in moments of crisis in her young life and how she had loved him then. In spite of the way he had deliberately hurt her now, she wanted to reach out to him. She found herself for some reason hoping with all her heart that Trevor hadn't been in love with her mother after all.

four

The rains came harder and lightning flashed, casting the Traum in an ominous glow. Its resemblance to a German castle, turreted and foreboding, added to its mystery. Elise dashed for the porch and felt the thrust of the wind slap sheets of rain against her legs. Inside the vestibule, she mopped the ends of her hair on her sleeve, dashing immediately toward the stairs. Her head ached, she was hungry and dripping wet, and she was in no mood to exchange pleasantries with the servants. She envisioned a raid on the pantry as soon as she was out of the soggy clothing.

Gripping the newel post, she glanced into the library and was surprised to see her father there, dozing in his leather chair. His head jerked as soon as he heard the creaking step. Elise paused, hoping he would resume his nap, but his eyes blinked open and focused on his daughter, while his fingers began drumming impatiently on the arm of the chair.

"It's about time you came home," he grumbled. "Where have you been?" He held his watch to the light and studied it.

Elise went slowly down the two steps and stood just inside the room. He stood and beckoned her to come closer, but she stayed where she was.

She blurted, "It started as a jaunt with Nettie and Justin but I spent most of the morning riding alone, thinking about what I want to do with my life." She had no intention of confiding her conversation with Trevor. Instead she added, "I didn't realize I went so far until I saw the storm coming. As you can see, I'm all wet." She hovered, ready to run for the stairs again.

"I've been waiting for you." The power behind his words detained her. "I didn't even go to the mill this morning. Come in. Come in." His voice was more pleasant now.

Elise stood her ground. "I was on my way to change out of these wet clothes and then raid the pantry. I'm famished."

"Come in." His request became firmer.

"Do you mind if I have a bite to eat first?"

"Yes, I mind," he said. "I don't like to be kept waiting."

"I could fix us both a tray and bring it here as soon as I change," she tried again, her mind racing through the conversation with Trevor.

"The servants prepared a tray for us over an hour ago."

"I wasn't aware you were expecting me." She felt her anger rise as she prepared to defend herself.

He ignored the remark. "A young lady of breeding does not run about the countryside dressed like a boy," he criticized.

"I have always dressed like this to ride. Everyone around here knows me. Besides, does it really matter?" Her voice was becoming husky. She hated her own weakness.

"In the future you will do what is expected of a young lady. Do I make myself clear?" He bit the end off a cigar and paused long enough to puff a cloud of blue smoke. "It was permissible to dress like a boy when you were a child, and though I never approved, your mother indulged you. But now it is different." He sent her a black look that closed both the subject and her mouth.

She sat on the edge of a chair looking indifferent, her defiance swallowed up by his commanding voice. She studied her hands, the pleats in her soggy trousers, the small tear in her jacket where she had encountered a bramble when she walked her horse down by the river. It was coming. The ultimatum was at hand. She sank deeper into her chair.

"You have an important meeting in the morning. I want you to be properly dressed and in the library by nine o'clock. Is that clear?" He waited for a sign from her. "Sit up straighter," he ordered. "And for heaven's sake, do something with that hair. You look a fright!"

"I was caught in the rain," she protested. Her lip quivered but she continued, "I have been home for less than a week and already you are making appointments without consulting me. Who is so important that we have to be presented at nine o'clock in the morning?"

"Not we. . .you. And I don't have to ask permission of my own daughter to arrange anything." He slammed his fist down on a table and she jumped.

She glared at him, her cheeks flushed. "Now that I am a woman, don't you think it would be a courtesy to ask me first?" She gave up thinking about food. One minute she was hot, the next cold. She felt faint and queasy, remembering how she had felt as child whenever she was disciplined. She hated it then, and she hated it now.

Wilhelm rose and closed the door. He leaned close to her to keep the conversation confidential. She opened her mouth to speak, but his hand shot out, slapping her across the face, silencing her instantly. He shrank back as though surprised by his own action.

Elise's hand covered her smarting cheek. She whispered

with loathing in her voice, "Papa, sometimes I hate you."
She matched his stare.

He raised his hand again. She sat unflinching, daring
him with her dark eyes. His hand poised in mid-air as he
reconsidered.

"In all my years you have hit me only once until today,"
she said hoarsely. "The first time was after Mamma died,
when I refuse to go to boarding school. Well, you had your
way that time, for I was too small to fight you. But I won't
forget that I had to become a woman to feel the back of
your hand again. Whatever it was you wanted to tell me it
will have to wait. I'm wet and hungry and have a headache
that would stop a train." She pronounced the last word
slowly as she watched his face.

He pushed her down in the chair as she started to get up.
"Aha, that's how it is," he said. "You've been listening to
rumors about the railroad. Well, now you will sit there and
listen to me. No daughter of mine will show me the disrespect you have since you came home from school. It seems
that keeping you in one of the country's finest institutions
has taught you only to defy your father."

"They taught us to think for ourselves, Papa. I thought
that is why I was sent away." She wondered what he would
have to say about Nettie thinking for herself, also.

"If disrespect is the end result, then I have wasted my
money." His words sounded tired, introspective.

Elise sensed a softening in her father's tone. She tried to
be remorseful. "I have so many questions to ask you, Papa,
but this is not the time."

"There is no better time. It is difficult to be alone these
days." He shrugged, however, mollified by her words.

She sighed. After a long moment the words spilled out,

"I have always wondered why you chose to send Nettie and me away, apart from each other. Don't you now how you broke our hearts?"

His fingers pushed against each other, and his eyes had a stare that didn't settle on Elise but upon a picture of Edwynna on the inside of his watch. Quietly, he explained, "I recognized something in Annette. She has always had her mother's temperament, but not her mother's wisdom. She needed a different training. You were always more pliable, more obedient. I chose the separate schools to suit you each best." He looked at her squarely. "I never expected you to come home on these terms, Lise."

Elise was touched. For the first time her father had called her by the pet name Nettie often used. She leaned forward and took the picture of her mother. She grasped his hand and held it firmly. "I never expected you to control all my thoughts my entire life, Papa."

"Nor do I expect to." He avoided her eyes. "I will let this pass as a bad moment for both of us." He patted her hand in a rare display of affection. "Now run along and change out of those dreadful clothes and feed yourself. No one can think on an empty stomach. But then I must insist you come back to me. We have much to discuss."

❧

Before Elise went looking for her father again she knelt by her bed and prayed. "Heavenly Father, forgive me for my defiance toward my father. I know he has only my best interest at heart. Let me bear with courage and strength the burdens You have set out for me."

She went slowly down to the library, her hair fastened with a ribbon, dressed now in a simple frock. Her face had the scrubbed look of a child. Not finding her father there, she searched the house, stopping to chat with Inger. At long last, she returned to her room to read while she waited for his return.

Evening had fallen before she found Wilhelm alone in the library. He made no apology for his absence but began the conversation as though there had been no interlude. "In the morning we have guests coming. I want you to meet the son of one of my friends." He walked to the fireplace and stood looking down at the unlit logs. The ornate mantel clock chimed quarter past seven.

Elise closed her eyes. Nettie had been right; the rumors were founded. The time had come to marry off the eldest daughter. Beads of perspiration stood on her upper lip. "I want no part of a planned life," she dared to say, her resolution to be a dutiful daughter gone.

He answered stiffly, "I thought you would prefer to meet the man you will marry before your wedding day. I have arranged a merger of families and businesses that will bring honor and prosperity to us and to Schiffley." He added proudly, "There will be wealth and position for you, also, Elise. So you see, I have considered you as well." He winked, making an attempt at levity. "Derrick Homes is an excellent choice for a mate. He has all the qualities needed to produce fine grandchildren, as you do."

"Derrick Homes!" She jumped to her feet. "Half the girls at school have spoken of what an arrogant brat he is, wild and self-centered. Oh, dear, I will have none of it," she cried.

"Elise!" She watched his face flush dark red.

"I won't do it," she insisted. "You can't make me."

"May I remind you, you are practically penniless, except for a pittance your mother left you. You can't expect your father to support you forever. Think of it, Elise. You will have a position of great esteem married to the son of a railroad baron. My silk mill will have links to the south and west." His eyes were fixed on a distant vision.

The absurdity of it struck Elise, and she threw her head back and laughed. "And who do you have waiting for Nettie? A steel magnate or some Persian prince?"

"Nettie will be snatched up at the appropriate time."

"I have to be matched up and Nettie will be snatched up," she said thoughtfully. "If I were more beautiful like my sister, you would take the chance of allowing me more choice, is that it?"

"You are the eldest. You will bring the most important . . .the railroad," he answered almost reverently.

Elise ran from the library in spite of her father's protests. In her room, she tore off her clothing and left it in a heap on the floor. Then she wrapped herself in a coverlet that had been hers as a child. Her head ached furiously. She lay curled up on the bed waiting for Nettie, all the while picturing Derrick Homes. At last, weariness took her into a deep dreamless sleep.

five

A small secretive noise woke her. Elise squinted at the dark figure in the doorway. The moonlight streaming in the window did little to identify the visitor. Still half asleep, she struggled to sit up.

"Nettie, is that you?" Her heart pounded.

"Be quiet, you'll wake Papa," was the answer that came through the darkness.

Elise relaxed, trying to get her thoughts together. "What are you doing?" She heard the rustle of silks and the soft plop-plop of slippers dropping onto the polished floor.

"I brought a nightgown from my room," Nettie whispered. "I want Papa to think I spent the night with you. Move over," she ordered as she slipped between the sheets. "We were talking over old times. Remember?" She giggled softly. Her body was warm from hurrying.

"Where have you been? It must be past midnight." Elise leaned on her elbow, glaring at her sister even though she couldn't see her.

"You sound just like Papa."

"Well? Where have you been?"

"I was walking in the moonlight if you must know."

"Whatever for?"

"I felt like it, all right? Justin and I went to a dance in Schiffley. It was such fun. I danced with boys I haven't seen since grade school. Afterward we went down to the lake. It's so beautiful in the moonlight. You should come

45

with us next time, Lise."

"No, thank you. I've had enough of being a third party."

"Don't tell me you're still mad about this morning," Nettie groaned.

"It's as good as forgotten," Elise snapped. "As long as we're awake, let's go down and get something to eat. Then you can tell me all about the dance. Does Papa know you went?"

"Of course not," she laughed. "That's what made it so much fun."

"You're impossible." Elise began crawling out over top of her. "Are you coming or not?"

"Well. . ."

"I promise I won't tell Papa."

"All right. I am rather hungry. All they served at the dance were the tiniest little sandwiches and watery lemonade." She yanked a wrapper from Elise's closet and they went down the back stairs to the kitchen, giggling like two young schoolgirls. Elise settled on a stool with a piece of chicken, and Nettie perched on a table with some fruit.

"Now tell me everything," Elise demanded.

Nettie hunched like a cat. "The dances are really fun, Lise. You must promise to go. I danced with one young chap who showed me the one-step. Oh, was he gorgeous! He had hair so close to his head it shown. And he had a moustache, too," she squealed. "I think he likes me. I hope I see him again."

"I can't picture Justin at a dance."

"He would only dance with me. He's shy, I guess, but you wouldn't think so the way he held my hand out on the lake."

"You were *on* the lake at midnight?" Elise asked incredulously.

"We were," said Nettie boastfully. "Justin assured me it would be all right. He brought along a torch for me to hold so he could see where we were going. It was beautiful."

"What's wrong with Justin? Papa will be furious. You could have drowned and no one would ever know."

"You said you wouldn't tell." Nettie sounded genuinely worried.

"Of course I won't, but there's little that escapes Papa."

Satisfied, Nettie jumped to her feet. "Why are we sitting in this drafty kitchen? We should be in bed."

Elise remained seated. "Papa was waiting for me when I came in from riding."

"So?"

"I cried myself to sleep and hardly ate all day." She was telling it badly, but she couldn't seem to make herself say the words. The prospect was just too terrible.

Nettie stood with her hands on her hips. "Are you going to tell me or do I have to drag it out of you?"

Elise sighed. "Coming home just isn't like I thought it was going to be."

"What do you mean?"

"I mean that at precisely nine o'clock this very morning I am to be presented to my future husband." Elise heard the words as though they were about someone else, though the pounding in her heart said otherwise.

Nettie gasped. "I was right." The whites of her eyes were distinctly visible in the candlelight.

"I'm to be sold like a sack of potatoes," Elise said dramatically. "And Papa is getting a railroad in exchange."

"A railroad! That's what he's wanted all his life! Well, I was right. It is time to be married off. I wonder who he has in mind for me."

Tears stung Elise's eyes to think that Nettie had so little concern for her sister's future. "He can't do this to me," she cried.

"Well, you have to get married sometime."

"Nettie!"

"What do you expect to do? Stay single all your life and become a spinster?"

"No, but I would like to pick my own husband," Elise argued.

"You know Papa is very continental. It's understandable he wants to make the match. At least he saw to it that you would be rich. I couldn't ask for more myself, though I do hope he doesn't get me an old codger."

"Money be burned." Elise covered her mouth. Even Nettie was surprised by her choice of words.

"You can fuss all you want, but I know this much about you, dear Elise—when the time comes for you to go down the aisle, you will do it with the man Papa has selected. What you do best in all this world is obeying Papa. And you will, till your dying day. It's the reason Papa is so sure of you."

Elise turned away, peering into the dark corners of the kitchen. Nettie was right. Everyone had always counted on her to do whatever they asked.

Wilhelm appeared in the doorway in a loose wooly robe which made him look much larger than he did in his black suit. "What are you doing down here at this hour? You will have the entire household awake with your cackling."

Nettie answered smoothly, "This sister of mine has quite an appetite. She got me awake to raid the pantry." She yawned and stretched sleepily. "We talked so late I decided to stay in her room for the night."

Wilhelm's eyes missed nothing, even in the candlelight. "Do you always wear shoes with your nightgown, Annette?" He pointed to the dancing slippers visible below her hem.

"I couldn't find my bedroom slippers so I took the first thing I could find."

Elise colored at Nettie's blatant lies. Why do you pass judgment on your sister, she thought, knowing in her heart that God was the one to Whom Nettie would have to answer for her lies.

Elise was glad for the dim light. "I never did get anything to eat before our little talk," she said quickly, though she hardly considered their conversation of little consequence. She would have to answer to God herself, she thought guiltily.

"I've been to Justin's room and he isn't there. My first thought was that you and he were out somewhere, Annette." Her father leaned close to her suspiciously. "I can't understand that young man. He prowls about, keeping dreadful hours. If only he had some interest in the business."

"But Justin is so good and thoughtful. He's devoted to you, Papa," Nettie was quick to defend.

Ignoring her remark, Wilhelm focused his attention on Elise. "It's time you were in bed, daughter. You have an important appointment in a few hours that will decide your destiny."

"I thought it had already been decided," she answered as her hands clenched and her stomach knotted. Dutifully, however, she led the procession up the back stairs.

Nettie followed Elise into her room and lay beside her on the narrow bed. Her deep breathing indicated she was soon asleep. She did not stir even when Elise got up from the bed and began to pace the floor.

જ

Nettie was sitting cross-legged on the foot of the bed when Elise finally awoke. "I'm surprised to see you slept so long, considering you have so little time until the witching hour."

"Perhaps sleep is the great escape. I want to run away." Elise was seriously considering the possibility.

"Where would you go?" Nettie suddenly looked wide awake.

"Perhaps Aunt Marguerite would take me in."

"Not unless you had a pocketful of money. You know how she loves money."

"We probably don't give her enough credit. You know how lost she was when Mamma died. It can't be easy losing your sister." Elise pushed aside the thought of losing Nettie.

"I have it." Nettie grasped her pillow and hugged it to her. Her dimples flashed as she peered impishly at Elise. "I've been sitting here for the last hour trying to concoct a plan." She fairly bounced off the bed. "Papa won't be looking for you in a disguise."

"A disguise?" Elise sat up, intrigued by the idea.

"If my plan works you will be under Papa's very nose and he won't recognize you." Nettie caught her sister's hands and pulled her out of bed.

Elise laughed, "Nettie, you are my salvation, next to the Lord, of course."

"We've got to work fast before the help gets started."

"Whatever you ask I will do. . .within reason," she hurried to add. "Oh, Papa thinks he has the upper hand in everything."

Nettie nodded soberly, pursing her lips. Then she began

giving orders. "You get these things from downstairs and I'll snatch a few up here. We'll meet back here in ten minutes."

"What's the disguise?" Elise whispered as she tiptoed to the door. "You haven't told me."

"That's the fun part. I must admit I never thought you were good for a prank. I'm proud of you, Lise." Nettie gave her a quick slap on the backside as she pushed her out the door.

Nearly a half hour later, the girls came together again. Nettie was breathless. She took clothing and a mop from a large cloth sack. In a matter of minutes, Elise was transformed into a scullery maid. Deftly, Nettie tied her hair up inside a dust cap and blackened one of her front teeth with the soot from the kitchen stove. Elise coughed and sputtered as a large soiled apron was added to her waist, and a smudge of soot on her cheek completed the picture.

Nettie walked around her creation, pulling a few wisps of hair from under the cap. She instructed Elise to wait in the closet lest someone came to summon them to breakfast. Then Nettie dashed to her room to dress for the day. Her face wore none of the look of guilt that Elise's did.

At exactly eight forty-five Elise set her knees to the flagstone entry just off the side porch. She took great deep breaths and plunged her arms into the cold soapy water, wishing Nettie had been able to find a hot kettle. She shivered and tested the stiff bristles in her hands. Very slowly, she began scrubbing the stones, one half at a time to make the task last the length of the visit.

The circular motion soon became rhythmic, having a soothing and relaxing effect on her. The water ran into the wide joints between the stones, filling tiny cracks. Back and forth she moved, mesmerized by the cleansing ritual. Her reddened hands dabbed at her itchy nose. More dark strands found their way from the edge of her cap. A sudsy spot appeared around her neck where the hair tickled. The only conscious thought in her mind was that she must keep her tongue from the bitter-tasting blackened tooth.

What had started as a prank soon became a personal purging, like the washing and scrubbing of her thoughts, the loathsome thoughts of marrying someone she didn't know or care to know. The brush flew from her fingers and streaked along the wainscoting. Angrily, she grabbed for it and sat back on her heels to ease her aching back. Someone spoke behind her, and she was almost thrown off balance by the unexpectedness.

A man tapped her shoulder. "Where might I find Miss Elise Waller?" he asked. "I have a message for her." There was a surly ring to his voice. His cheeks were puffy and he had an unmanly smooth skin. He stood looking down, impatiently snapping his fingers.

"How should I know where Miss Waller is?" Elise retorted with a nasal twang. "You can see what I'm up to." She avoided the eyes that glared at her, proud that she had mimicked his speech so well.

"Tart." He pushed her in the middle of the back and she slipped across the wet stones. From there she got a better look at her assailant. The yellow glass around the door cast a sickly light on his already sallow complexion.

"Let me give you a hand." He reached out.

She extended her hand, glad to see he was being a gentleman. Instead, he yanked her to the first step where he tried to kiss her. She bit his hand.

"You don't have to act prissy with me, miss. Now I want

you to look for Elise Waller and tell her she is expected in the library."

She brought the bristles of the brush up hard against his chin. He winced in pain and brushed water from his suit. He raised his hand to slap her.

A door opened down the hall and footsteps approached. Quickly, the man was gone, but not before he had set her down into the bucket of cold water. Elise sat there sobbing.

A familiar face bent over her and helped her to her feet. She stared into Trevor's eyes, desperately wanting a place to escape. He began reassuring her, and Elise realized he didn't recognize her. Finally, she stopped crying and tried to answer his questions. She was acutely aware of his protective arm about her shoulder.

"You must know there are many who would take advantage of a serving girl, especially one as pretty as you. Let's sit down on the steps and calm you down. Would you like a glass of water?"

She shook her head vehemently.

He took her shaking hand and began talking to her in a soothing way she hadn't heard since he had found her at her mother's grave when she was a child. His words were kind and full of sympathy.

"He didn't actually harm you, did he?"

She shook her head, not wanting the moment to end, breathing in the leathery smell that was always about him.

"Learn to work with someone else. It will protect you." He took out a large handkerchief and began wiping the smudges from her face. She grabbed at it and dabbed weakly at her face lest the disguise be removed.

"Don't trouble yourself, sir," she said hoarsely.

A door burst open down the length of the hall and some-one called her name. She stood up uncertainly and so did Trevor.

"I'll be on my way so I don't cause trouble for you with the housekeeper. Keep your chin up, girl."

For a second she stared after him as he let himself out the side door. Then she dashed to her room where she fell weeping on the bed. The indignities of the game had not been anticipated. She reached for the note the brute had shoved in her pocket.

"I desperately want to meet you, Elise," she read. It was signed, "Derrick." She threw the note across the room. If he was like his messenger she never wanted to meet him. She clutched Trevor's handkerchief to her cheek.

Cool reason began to return. Her father's punishment would be severe if she didn't go downstairs immediately. The prank served nothing more than to humiliate her and made no difference to the outcome. She brushed her hair and searched through her closet. She could find nothing there that would make her look awful enough to meet the man she didn't want to marry.

The door of the room flew open wide and Nettie bounded in. "Papa's furious. He sent word you have five minutes or he will send you to the mill to work. He's like a raging bull when he's mad, Lise. Hurry! You can't possibly think this would be worse than one of those silk mills. I've heard the horror stories of how girls lose their arms in those monster machines and live in those awful boarding houses." Nettie's face mirrored the terror of it.

"You're exaggerating, Nettie." If only her sister knew the indignities she had suffered from their childish prank.

Nettie selected a more becoming dress for Elise and a

matching ribbon for her hair. "This is sure to please Papa." Her fingers shook as she tied the bow.

"For someone who is about to drop some rather unpleasant news on Papa yourself, you are going out of your way to make sure I pass the test. Or have you changed your mind?"

Nettie dabbed some powder under Elise's eyes to cover the redness. "No, I haven't changed my mind," she said calmly. She stood back and squinted. "You have too much color to use the rouge. Don't forget I want to hear all the details."

Elise took Trevor's rumpled handkerchief from the bed and tucked it into her waist. Her heart pounded on each step downstairs. Outside the study door, she tried to collect herself by taking a big breath and letting it out slowly. She felt the bulge of the handkerchief in her shirtwaist. It gave her the courage to open the door.

The library was crowded and thick with the smell of cigars and body odor. Elise looked neither right nor left but proceeded directly to her father's desk. She was aware of the presence of several men in the room. They had stopped speaking when she walked in the room. She stood waiting for her father to stop fuming and acknowledge her.

Wilhelm's face was flushed. He avoided her eyes when he finally stood up. He lifted a large stein of beer, sloshing it on the desktop as he gestured grandly to introduce his daughter.

Elise turned and curtsied to a man with an orange-colored beard. Their eyes met. His smile was pleasant and his face kindly with a devilish wink. His portly body was short when he stood to take her hand firmly in his. For some reason she took an instant liking to him and was relieved when he was introduced as her prospective father-in-law. He offered his arm and she accepted, glad to have someone to lean upon. One by one she met the other men in the party, a future uncle, Derrick's cousin, their attorney. At last she stared into the eyes of the messenger who had accosted her in the hallway. She stepped back in surprise as Mr. Homes patted her hand gently and introduced his son Derrick.

Elise opened her mouth to protest. At that precise moment a yawn escaped her lips. Derrick blinked and pointed to the blackened tooth still in her mouth. He let out a guffaw and held his sides with laughter. His father and uncle joined his merriment. Soon the room was filled with raucous laughter. It was then that Elise collapsed before the Homes men and her startled father.

&

She came to when a spurt of water was poured on her from her father's desk. Someone helped her sit up and the water trickled down her back. Derrick stood above her with amusement on his face. The hatred in her eyes was veiled by her long thick lashes. Her father's bewildered expression confirmed that he had not been informed of her indiscretion.

While Elise was being helped to her feet, Wilhelm was attending to business. With much fanfare, he carried the ink stand to the desk and opened an official-looking document. He dismissed his daughter from the room, gesturing brusquely. As the door closed behind her, the sound of muffled laughter filled her ears.

On rubbery legs, she broke into a run as soon as she felt the cool air of the foyer. Panic filled her as her stomach surged. She became instantly sick into the potted ferns.

She tried to wipe the bitterness from her mouth as she dragged herself to her room. Derrick's leering face seemed to float on every step. Alone in her room, she sank gratefully to the floor. Once, Nettie peered in, but she quickly closed the door again.

Wilhelm found her an hour later. He lifted her to the bed and covered her. He was acutely aware of her pallor and the frailty of her body in her best blue dress.

six

The early morning was exceptionally dreary as Elise sat on the front porch step and waited for her father. Mist hung heavily in the air and dampened her spirits as well as her clothing. She hugged her shawl more closely. Her stomach knotted as she tucked her feet under the hem of her skirt. The tiny gold watch on the chain about her neck said it was only two minutes later than when she had looked at it before.

At last the door opened and closed behind her. Wilhelm hesitated only a moment before he stepped gingerly around her and on down the steps to the drive. The hour was precisely six-thirty, and he was on schedule as usual. He paused and glanced at his daughter who stood on the second step and met his eyes on an equal level.

"I have to talk to you, Papa."

"Why not at breakfast? Not here in the driveway."

"There's hardly any privacy with all the clamor of breakfast," she laughed with a forced, unnatural sound.

"Elise, I know exactly what is on your mind. I have told you the agreement is ironclad and cannot be broken, even if I wanted to, which I don't. There is no turning back. You also gave your consent, if you recall. The only way to escape is if I go back on my word, and you know how I keep my word." His voice was firm.

Vehemently, she shook her head. "That was not my intention, Papa, to talk of the marriage. However, I would like a word with you, alone in your study." She felt like she was asking for an audience with a king.

"It must be very important to get you out of bed this early." He checked his pocket watch, squinting in the mist to make out the hands. "I'm a trifle behind schedule now so I can give you only a few minutes." Turning abruptly, he led the way to the library where he closed the door and stood waiting.

Elise ran to the window and opened the drapes. The center of the room was bathed in bluish light, but the bookcases and chairs remained in the shadows.

"Papa, I have a favor to ask of you," she began timidly, waiting for him to respond.

He tugged at his beard. "Daughter, you know I rarely grant favors or bargains. For that's what they usually turn out to be ... bargains. However, since you are my flesh and blood I will at least hear you out. I did promise you a few minutes." He sighed. "I still think it has to do with Derrick Homes."

Elise clapped her hands to her cheeks. "You are wrong, Papa, but in a way you are right, too."

"I have no time for riddles—besides, I loathe them. On with it. Your time is running out." He toyed impatiently with his pocket watch.

"Take me into your business, Papa," she blurted. "Show me how it operates and let me be a part of it so I may help you."

Were Wilhelm a man of humor he would have laughed in the face of such a proposal. As it was he simply shook his head at the absurdity of it. "Do you know what you are asking? Why, it's unheard of."

"I realize Justin has no interest in the mill, but I would

like to learn, Papa. I would make you proud." She looked up at him with pleading in her eyes.

"Out of the question. You would get no respect from the men who supervise the operations or from the girls who run the machines. They would resent a woman's presence in a man's world. That will be your husband's place, not yours." He sighed again. "Was there something else on your mind?" he asked, dismissing the subject as though it had never been mentioned.

Elise sat in one of the stiff chairs and leaned back into the shadows. Only her white hands were focused in the light. "If you won't have me in the mill, perhaps you would give me permission to live on the lower farm and raise horses. They have always been my first love. I know I could manage a farm."

"You are to be wed any day now, Elise. What will all this prove to be except a waste of time?"

She leaned forward into the arc of light and caught his gaze with her earnest brown eyes. "Papa, I want you to promise me that I can have my freedom until my eighteenth birthday next April." A wisp of cool air stirred in the room. "I don't recall a date on the agreement you signed."

He stepped back as though she had handed him a blow. "So, I was right all along," he hissed.

"I don't find this request at all unreasonable. I can have some time to get better acquainted with Derrick and learn some useful work so I may help him in the future. Please, Papa."

"No daughter of mine is going to attend to the breeding of animals," he said sourly.

"Then there is one thing I might do—with your help, of

course," she said quietly as though weighing each word before she dropped it on him.

He sniffed suspiciously, recognizing the smugness on her face. He realized he had been led to this very moment. "Which is precisely the reason you detained me this morning. Your mother used to use the same tactics. I would have thought Nettie would be the one to use this ploy but I suppose you inherited equally, though it was Nettie who inherited her looks."

The unexpected mention of her mother stopped Elise short. She bit back stinging tears that had sprung to her eyes. After all the years of comparing herself to Nettie's looks, she had been sure nothing of her mother's had been left to her. She could hardly fathom that any of her mother's temperament could be hers after all.

Slowly, she composed herself and began to speak, so softly Wilhelm strained to hear her words. "It is strange that you should mention Mother when what I want most is to begin her work again. She helped so many. They still speak of it years later. I want to help the women and children who live in poverty. Oh, Papa, they have such wretched lives. There is little education or medicine now that Dr. Nevitt will close his practice."

"They will soon have a doctor," Wilhelm was quick to point out. "I have sent a contribution to help finance Trevor's equipment myself," he boasted.

"And that is so good of you, Papa," she flattered, all the while remembering that she had learned her father had withdrawn support from Trevor's medical school expenses, forcing the town's people to meet the costs. "But the children need better education and the women need to be taught hygiene. What I want is an allowance to help them," she said firmly.

"I will discuss it with Derrick's family." His hand poised on the doorknob.

"No." She stood up and shouted, a sound that reverberated through the library. At that moment the sun came out and slashed the furniture in white light, exposing the shadows and the little particles of dust suspended in the air. Wilhelm dropped his hand from the knob and with it any thought of leaving.

"This is between you and me." Her eyes blazed. "I want an agreement before the wedding—or there will be no wedding." She sucked in her breath, surprised at her own audacity.

Wilhelm sat down at his desk with a look of defeat. "Very well, you shall have your allowance."

"Put it in writing, like all the agreements you make." She handed him the pen from the ink stand.

As he wrote, Wilhelm was totally unaware of Elise's white knuckled hands as they gripped that chair back, or the pallor that had come to her face.

"You drive a hard bargain, daughter." He met her unflinching gaze.

"Not nearly as hard as yours, Papa. Your bargain will change the rest of my life, forever. In spite of what you think, I am your daughter, not a piece of property to be bartered."

He studied her for a moment. "What makes you stay, Elise?" he asked in a whisper. "You could have run away like lots of young girls. They do it every day."

"I'm not quite sure. Perhaps to prove I'm as worthy as a son. Perhaps I have been called by God to help these people. I have to make sure before I deny God—or you." Her lips tensed and her words trailed off.

Wilhelm put the blotter to the paper and handed it to her. "Your eighteenth birthday," he said. Then he closed his eyes to the sights around him.

Elise left the room with only a faint click of the door. She stood outside the door feeling the stiff paper between her fingers. For the first time in her life she had questioned her father's authority. Her hands shook and her breath came in short gasps. She felt a strange sense of elation.

&

The night of the engagement party was accompanied by a flurry of activity never before witnessed in the Traum. The staff was astir with the changing of draperies, polishing silver, and moving furniture to make way for the dancers. The windows were cleaned to a shine, though no one was expected to look out of them except to the lanterns which decorated the terrace and grounds. In the great hall the woodwork and floors had been polished to a fine patina. Ice chests containing exotic foods were stacked in the kitchen and the ice house. The back porch was laden with an assortment of serving dishes, linens, and utensils. Milling about were caterers under the specific directions of the French chef who had been hired to oversee the preparation of food and drink. New maids, hired just for the occasion, were issued uniforms and given instructions on serving guests. Among the last to arrive was a handsomely costumed gentleman who would formally introduce the guests as they made their entrances to the gala celebration.

Wilhelm had thought of everything and spared no expense to impress his future partner. He supervised each minute detail, insisting on perfection. He even had the audacity to invade the sanctity of the chef's domain, inspecting and tasting the food and passing judgment.

The musicians arrived late in the afternoon and began rehearsing in the alcove just off the dining room. At precisely seven-thirty, they were instructed to take their places on the small stage in the main hall that had been especially built to accommodate them. From this vantage point their melodic strings would fill the house and the night with music.

Arrangements had been made to handle the overflow of carriages and vehicles that would gather in front of the mansion. Though many attending the party would come in carriages drawn by fine horses, some were expected to arrive in engine-driven vehicles. Trevor Lucas was hired to tend to the horses, and another man was given the task of keeping automobiles off the spacious lawn and away from the animals.

From Schiffley, great crowds of people came and stood along the driveway just to see the elegant guests as they arrived and to hear the strains of music as it drifted from the Traum into the night air. They danced on the green and shared cakes and punch that the host had graciously sent, creating their private party, milling about the lawn and standing on tiptoe to peer through the sparkling windows for a glimpse of the dancers and the guests of honor.

Even Inger rose to the occasion. After watching her trying to make a gown from discarded velvet drapes, Wilhelm had sent for a designer, and ball gowns were made for the women. A hairdresser came from Philadelphia to copy the latest styles. Nettie and Inger had setting lotion applied to give sheen to their curls, but Elise declined and wore her hair loosely about her shoulders after it had been brushed to a natural shine.

Nettie ran back and forth between their rooms and fussed about wearing a sash, and how to comb her sticky hair now that the lotion had dried. She rummaged through the glove box and fretted over the length of the gloves and whether they were needed at all. Her minor tantrums received little sympathy from Elise who was preoccupied with the matter of getting herself down the long stairs on extremely shaky legs. Under the circumstances, her sister's problems seemed petty and over-inflated.

Nettie ran to the window overlooking the driveway. "They're here," she said with excitement in her voice, her face flushed. "The Homes family has arrived in four automobiles." She fanned herself. "The men are in tails and the women are wearing furs. Oh, can you believe it? Furs in September." She sank to the window seat. "Oh, Lise, aren't you the least bit excited?" She jumped up and pulled Elise along to a small spot on the balcony where they could watch the guests arrive without being seen from below. Nettie had never outgrown the habit of peering down as guests came into the house.

Elise said, "I remember Mamma standing there, greeting people, her hair piled up on her head, her gown more splendid than any of the guests." Nettie didn't comment. They were each remembering bits and pieces of the past.

The Homes family stood together to await their introductions. Nettie grabbed for her sister's arm. "Is that him?" she gasped.

Elise nodded and a chill ran down her spine. She shivered involuntarily.

"Lise," Nettie sighed, "he's so handsome. You never told me. How can you possibly be unhappy? Oh, let me be the one to seal the merger," she pleaded, drawing her hand dramatically across her brow.

"Father wouldn't hear of it. The oldest is first according to the rules, I've been reminded. Besides, you always exaggerate, Nettie." She couldn't help laughing at her sister as Nettie swooned on the carpet.

Nettie sat up quickly. "I mean it, dear Lise. Let me be the one to make the sacrifice," she begged on her knees.

"Just remember, Nettie, looks are deceiving. Derrick is his father's darling. Mr. Homes really wants to make a man of the spoiled brat. Papa won't be too happy with him as a son-in-law, other than bringing the railroad into the deal. He's a bully and a cheat."

"He wasn't cheating on you, Lise. You hadn't even met him yet when he tried to kiss the servant girl. He had no way of knowing it was you."

Elise grimaced. "Anyway, Nettie, I'm surprised you are ready to think of marriage."

"Make no mistake about me," Nettie agreed. "I want to have some fun first." She dashed back to her room, calling something over her shoulder that was lost in her haste.

Justin came from his room, looking elegant in his formal black tie and tails, taller and thinner than before. He blocked Elise's passage to her room.

"What a wonderful opportunity," he said, smiling down at her.

"I have no idea what you're talking about, Justin. Let me pass, please."

He reached for her hand and held it against his cheek. "Dear sister, I wish you the best." He began squeezing her hand until she winced with pain. "May I take this moment to ask. . .no, demand, that you be a dutiful daughter and do your Papa proud. Give him the gift he wants more than anything. . .the railroad." He paused and the line around his mouth hardened. "Be a good girl and don't disappoint us." He dropped her hand as though it were a dead fish and went on downstairs.

Elise blinked back tears of indignation. She walked slowly to her room. Weighted heavily by emotion, she opened the door to her closet and plucked the pale blue silk from the hanger. She studied it at arm's length.

Rows of ruffles covered the hem and seed pearls draped across the bodice and around the waist. Her father himself had selected the design and chosen the color to complement her hair and complexion. It reminded her of gossip among the servants that he had selected all of Edwynna's and the children's clothing. Inger's coming had changed all of that, if indeed, it were true. He accepted his new wife's staid practical tastes with no comment.

Nettie ran back into the room and snatched the gown from her sister's hand. She stood in front of the long oval mirror, swaying slightly to the strains of the music, with the dress held in front of her. "Your dress is so beautiful, Lise. I wish Papa had chosen that color for me. It goes with my eyes." She threw the dress on the bed and looked at herself. "Look at this gown. I hate it. Its so plain. I even tried it with a sash and gloves. I still hate it." She tugged at the small puffed sleeves. "It makes me look like a child."

Elise sat on the bed and toyed with the rows of pearls. She made no move to put her dress on.

Nettie moved to the window again. "They're still arriving. I can't imagine the house will hold so many people." She craned her neck. "Trevor is being kept busy. I'm sure he will be glad to open his practice and leave all of this behind so he won't have to be anyone's servant anymore.

He must hate it."

"But a doctor is a servant, Nettie. He will always be a servant to the people who need him." Elise joined her sister at the window and recognized Trevor in the lamplight as he moved easily between the horses. Once she thought he glanced up at her window, and she pulled Nettie back.

Impulsively, Elise picked up the dress and held it out to Nettie. "You like it so much, why don't you wear it instead? I prefer the rose-colored silk. It suits me more. Although I must say I hope it doesn't match my eyes." They laughed together.

Nettie stopped short, realizing Elise was dead serious. "But Papa is expecting you to wear it."

Elise's chin jutted out the same way Nettie's had when she spoke of not returning to school. "Never mind what Papa expects," she said. "It's good we are the same size. Let's switch."

She didn't need to make a second request. Nettie seized the dress and put it on excitedly, at last admiring herself in the mirror. "Oh, thank you, thank you, Lise," she whispered.

"There are stars in your eyes tonight, Nettie," Elise said softly. "This party should be for you."

"In a way it is for both of us," Nettie answered with more than usual insight. "Papa has something in mind for me, also. Maybe tonight I will meet the man I am to marry." She pinched her cheeks and ran her hands over her small waist.

Wistfully, Elise watched her sister. "It's a lovely gown and you do it justice, Nettie. It just wasn't right for me. I'm glad you decided to wear it."

She looked past her sister to her own reflection. The

rose dress was simple and subdued but not at all unattractive. Her hair cascaded loosely down her back, and her face was young and smooth, with the beguiling look of innocence. Only a thread of regret gleamed in her eyes for the decision to play second best to her beautiful sister. No matter, she thought. There was no turning back. Justin was right. She would be the dutiful daughter and obey Papa's wishes.

She stood up and took a deep breath. She reached for Nettie's arm. "Let's go downstairs together."

Nettie gaped in surprise. "But Papa wants you to make a grand entrance. That's the way we rehearsed it."

"Please, Nettie, for one more time we shall be sisters in the sun."

"What a strange thing to say, Lise. We will always be sisters." She looked at Elise uncertainly.

"In all of life there is sunshine and shadow," Elise said. "This will be one of the moments to remember, when we walk downstairs to beautiful music among friends and family. By the time we reach the bottom of the stairs one of us will be deep in the shadows. There may be no more sunshine to warm us both at the same time. Remember this moment, Nettie. I want to share it with you." Her eyes were dry and clear and she paused only a moment on the top step as the music rose to meet them.

seven

The music paused, then began again on a crescendo note as the girls started down the spiral staircase. A hush fell over the guests as they clustered about, watching as the girls came arm in arm. When they came into full view, they were loudly cheered and applauded.

Wilhelm winced. His annoyance was short-lived, however, for he began to realize he was a fortunate man as he watched the young men and their fathers admiring Nettie. He was also pleased by the way Inger had risen to the occasion, mingling freely and speaking easily to the guests. She was still attractive, looking handsome and regal with the glittering tiera on her swirl of dark blond hair.

Instinctively, Elise looked for her father, fearing the worst because of the change in dresses. The smile froze on her face when she saw his eyes fixed upon Nettie. The distant look said he was remembering another time, another woman. For a moment she glanced at her sister and caught a glimpse of the past. Quickly, she looked back to her father in time to see his eyes narrow and close. When he opened them again, he glared at Elise.

Those assembled at the bottom of the stairs saw the contrast between the sisters, but less acutely than Wilhelm had. Words of admiration escaped the lips of men and women alike. That the sisters should make their entrance together seemed only natural. They complemented each other, one fair, the other dark, well matched in height, the same tilt of their heads, the similar features. Their eyes and skin tones set them apart, one dark the other fair. Nettie's gowns was more sparkling and adorned, Elise's more tasteful. One simple jewel at her throat did more to complement her than all the pearls on Nettie's bodice. Not all eyes were on Nettie.

For a brief second Elise caught sight of Trevor where he had come to stand by the open door. In an instant he was gone and she was not sure she had really seen him.

The girls had scarcely made their way around the ballroom when a note was passed. Wilhelm's attention was diverted from his daughters as he quickly read the slip of paper and whispered something to Inger. They put their heads together, and then Wilhelm threaded his way to the library with a decided lack of urgency. In fact, he dawdled among his guests, greeting old friends, pausing by his daughters where he beamed proudly, lingering near them before the rush of young men who came to fill their dance cards. He had not missed Derrick's presence in Nettie's line.

The young nephew of Randall Homes came forward again and tugged on Wilhelm's sleeve.

"Sir, Uncle Randall has taken himself to your library to meet with you there in a few minutes. . .at your convenience, of course." The lad's words were spoken distinctly, but nevertheless were drowned by the music and laughter. He repeated them and Wilhelm nodded in understanding, though if the truth be known, he had heard perfectly the first time.

He dismissed the boy with a wave of his hand. His eyes met Inger's above heads and across the width of the room. He frowned and extricated himself from a group of acquaintances. In the hallway he ducked into one of the salons and sat on a blue velvet settee where he indulged himself with a few puffs of a new cigar. After a time he stood up, straightened his tie, and walked confidently from the room. Even then he did not feel compelled to hurry.

In the library, Wilhelm found Randall Homes pacing the floor. The young messenger was untidily sprawled across the leather couch. At the sight of Wilhelm he made a hasty exit, leaving the two men facing each other.

"Randall." Wilhelm offered his hand and his most pleasant voice. "I believe you wish to speak to me."

The small man grasped Wilhelm's hand, then stood waiting for him to be seated. Wilhelm stood for awhile, running his fingers across his gleaming desktop.

"This desk was once owned by Lincoln," he explained. "Everything on it is a collection from the Civil War. I was not in America during the war and who won it is really immaterial to me, but I have always admired men fighting for a cause. Fighting for what they believe in is a sign of good men. My homeland has been through centuries of destruction which would make your Civil War pale by comparison. The real losers in my country were those who would not lift a finger to overthrow the invaders. So you see, we have been either fighters or losers. Let me assure you, Mr. Homes, I am a fighter." With that emphatic remark he took his seat, leaning forward in his chair, taking into account his future partner's nervous posture. "Was there something you wished to discuss with me before I make my announcement? I'm sure my daughter is having her share of anxiety over the delay, especially since your son is dancing every dance with her sister." Wilhelm's smile froze on his face as he waited for an answer.

The red beard twitched. Homes's eyes were hooded, his remarks cautious when he finally spoke. He raised his gaze to Wilhelm and matched him stare for stare. "Derrick is so captivated with your younger daughter he requests the agreement may be altered to have her hand instead of Miss Elise." His offer sounded offhand. His eyes remained steady.

Wilhelm sent a puff of thick smoke across the desk, and Randall was forced to blink several times. "But that is not possible, sir. Nettie is not quite fourteen and her hand will not be offered for some time," he lied, straightfaced.

Randall suppressed his indignation. "She told my son she is nearly sixteen. A few months longer is of no consequence to a merger such as ours." Homes flicked some imaginary lint from his coat sleeve.

Wilhelm laughed. "The child is willful. She has been known to stretch the truth."

Homes declined a cigar from the aromatic smelling box. "I understand there was a slight misunderstanding between my son and Miss Elise. For some reason he was under the impression she had been impersonating a servant." He smiled weakly.

Wilhelm was not smiling when he slammed the lid of the cigar box. "Both my daughters have been known to play pranks on occasion."

"My son is so taken with Miss Annette, he insists he will have no other," Homes said. "Of course our merger will go ahead as planned. Only the bride will change." This time Randall was the one laughing as he watched Wilhelm grow red with fury.

"Very well, then." Wilhelm sat back and folded his hands across his vest. "We shall have no merger." His eyes narrowed on the mahogany panels above Randall's head.

The little man stood, fingering his watch pocket. "I will discuss your ultimatum with my son." All color had drained from his face. He took long strides with his short legs, leaving the door standing open behind him.

Inger poked her head around the door only minutes after he had left. "*Wass is loss?*" Her tongue always slipped into her native German when she was anxious.

"Calm yourself, Inger." He rose to extend a chair. "They are bluffing. Well, so am I. They have no idea how much we need their railroad. They believe I am only thinking of my daughters."

"What are you saying?" She sat rigid on the edge of the chair.

"Young Homes wants Annette instead of Elise. If he was smart he would insist on Elise. She will bring more to the marriage than Nettie ever could, but at this moment it depends upon how much his father wants a partnership in my silk mill." He sat back with half a smile crinkling the lines above his dark beard. "The merger will benefit him as well as me. I have not spent hours on the widow's walk at the top of the house for nothing. I know how many trips his trains make through the valley and how many cars are empty. I understand more about shipping than he gives me credit for."

Inger stood up and shook her husband's hand across the desk. "I never doubted for a minute that you could strike a deal, Wilhelm. Our Justin could be a manager of a fine company like a railroad."

Wilhelm pulled his beard. "My mill is also a fine company and Justin will not work for me. He wants only to take," he complained. "He is a scholar he says. What does one do with a scholar? This is not the time to even consider a position on the railroad."

There was silence in the room. Wilhelm slumped into his chair. Inger studied her fingernails.

The door burst open and Randall Homes came in, red-faced and puffing. He glanced at Inger and she immediately left the room. He knotted his hands behind his back. "After reconsideration my son has agreed to your terms. You may make the announcement of his betrothal to Miss Elise. He asks only your indulgence and forgiveness for his conduct this evening." He coughed dryly and reached across the desk to offer his hand in another seal of agreement. As quickly as he had come, he left.

Wilhelm remained seated. He took a large handkerchief from his pocket and began mopping his forehead and neck. Beads of perspiration stood out on the backs of his hands, and he dabbed at them. Then, in the total silence of the room, he threw his head back and laughed until tears ran down his cheeks. He puffed violently on his cigar until he was enveloped in a white haze. He coughed until the spittle flew from his mouth. Finally, he relaxed and began to envision the transportation of his silks throughout the United States. His mill would grow and expand beyond belief. If he had to share some of that wealth with his new partner, then so be it. The company would always bear the Waller name. He had seen to that.

He paused a moment by his desk, smoothing a Northern emblem with his large fingers. He treasured the moment, likening it to the possible elation of the North when the treaty was signed in a strange sounding place called Appomatox Court House. He pictured uniforms and trumpets and polished swords raised in salute to brave men, and for one more time in his life he was glad to be counted among the victors.

રે

The orchestra stopped playing halfway through a waltz as Wilhelm took the second step at the end of the ballroom, putting him well above his guests. He raised a glass above his head as he called for attention. On his right, Inger looked more flustered than she had all evening. A crowd quickly gathered about them.

"Ladies and gentlemen, I ask your attention, please." He was flushed with excitement as he began to command their attention. He swayed slightly and laughed easily and boisterously. When there was a reasonable silence, he continued, "It gives Mrs. Waller and myself a great deal of pleasure to make an announcement." He winked broadly at Inger who blushed a beet red. Her tiara was slightly askance on her head. Over the sea of faces he saw Nettie come in from the terrace. She was extremely pale. In a few moments she had slipped into the crowd and was lost from her father's view.

Wilhelm focused his attention on Elise. All eyes followed his gaze to the somber but attractive young woman. The onlookers parted, and father and daughter stood staring at each other.

"My dear girl, on this night, is bringing to the Waller family a gift of note. There will be a merger of families and businesses which will bring prosperity to our house and our beloved Schiffley. It comes to us by way of the Homes Railroad Empire. Elise, I am pleased to announce, is now betrothed to Derrick Homes." From all sides there were cheers and applause.

In spite of the flush that came to her face, Elise felt a chill sweep through her body. How like her father to consider the merger before the marriage. Even in the announcement of her marriage he could hardly contain the elation of his personal victory. Feeling nauseated and faint, she focused on her father to overcome her humiliation.

Wilhelm gestured grandly, nearly falling off the step. "And now, may I present the betrothed couple, my daughter Elise and her future husband, Mr. Derrick Homes, of the Homes Railroad Empire."

Cheers filled the room as Derrick came out of a small salon just off the ballroom. He bowed in front of Elise and took her hand. Ceremoniously, he placed a glittering sapphire on her finger and proudly held it up for all to see.

Elise smelled his garlic breath as he leaned forward to kiss her. Blackness tunneled in on her until she felt smothered and sick. Quickly, she excused herself and ran to the salon that Derrick had just come from. He smiled and waved to the guests. "We will be out to greet all of you as soon as my bride-to-be regains her composure." With that remark he gave a sly wink and closed the door behind them.

Elise was seated in a small wingback chair fanning herself with a lace handkerchief. From a small table he poured water from a crystal decanter and handed her the glass, spilling a portion onto the front of her dress.

Clenching his teeth, he said, "I guess we will just have to make the best of it, Elise. There is no getting out of a contract with your father. Lord knows, I tried." He sighed. "You and I are not the only ones disappointed."

"What do you mean?" She looked up as he towered above her.

"Never mind. The opportunity is past."

"I feel this is some kind of dream I cannot wake from. Perhaps God is trying to tell me something."

"Oh, it's a dream all right, but not from God. The father is your own, not a heavenly one." He threw himself in a chair opposite hers. "Just what kind of simple game were you playing the day we met? Surely you didn't believe it would change anything? Our fathers are hard-driven men." His words were barely a whisper as he glanced toward the door. "If we are both unhappy there must be a way out." He grabbed her hand and held it tightly. "I am my father's son. I know without question what this merger means to him. We will do as we are told, make no mistake about it."

She held her head high. "I am as much my father's daughter as you are your father's son."

"Then we should have no conflict. We have yet to seal our bargain." He pulled her to him and kissed her roughly on the lips.

Justin looked into the room in time to see his sister recoil from the kiss and turn away. He smiled and quietly closed the door.

&

For a long time after all was quiet in the house Elise wandered alone on the terrace. She replayed the events of the evening in her mind until she wanted to scream. She closed her eyes and hugged her arms in her rose gown. She couldn't sleep, even her prayers faltered, confusing her father's will with the Lord's. Sometimes she thought they were one in the same. Her father was playing God, even though he professed not to believe in Him. She had never wanted to admit he could be telling the truth about his lack of faith, but now she didn't know.

A figure moved on the lawn and she stepped back into the shadows, surprised that anyone was out on the grounds. The stranger came across the lawn and up the steps confidently, as though he knew she was there. Elise jumped when he spoke.

"I saw you clearly in the moonlight, Elise." Trevor's voice came across the shadows and found her hiding there. "I'm sorry. I didn't mean to startle you. Is anything wrong?"

She stepped into the moonglow and held her arms tightly to her body. "What. . .what are you doing here?"

"I just finished with the last of the horses. It's been a long night. I thought no one was about. There *is* something wrong," he said flatly.

"No. . .yes," she admitted. "It's not something I can talk about, though. I must go in."

"Wait," he detained her. "They tell me tonight was a special occasion. Congratulations, Elise. I hope you will be very happy." His tone was not as light as his words.

She wished she could see his face to read the truth in his dark eyes. "You don't know. . ."

"You are to be a grand lady. This is what you wanted."

"I never told you or anyone that." A sob came with her protest and she turned and ran to the house and up to her room. His words tore at her heart. She stood outside her door before going into the bedroom. Her breath caught in sharp gasps.

As she entered the room she saw that Nettie lay awake on the cot beside Elise's bed. Still, Elise tiptoed, hope to avoid a confrontation with her sister. She had been disturbed that her sister had avoided her all evening, but she didn't want to make a scene tonight. They were both tired. She struggled with the sash on her dress in the dim light that glowed from a small lamp on the dressing table. In exasperation, she knocked over a bottle of perfume, and it broke on the floor. She ran to open the window as the odor became overpowering.

"I wish you would be more careful."

"I'm sorry, Nettie. I thought you would be asleep. I know something is bothering you." Trevor's hint of concern washed over her. He knew there was something wrong, too. "We have to talk. Remember how we promised to have no secrets? I can't imagine what you have to feel badly about." Words spilled out in spite of her resolve. "You had the prettiest gown. You were the belle of the ball. No one was any lovelier than you, Nettie. And you weren't the one being sold into marriage."

Nettie yawned. "I'm too tired to discuss the party, Lise. There's nothing to talk about anyway." She turned over and the cot groaned. "I'll never sleep on this monstrosity. I hope whatever guest has my bed tonight appreciates the sacrifice I made giving up my bed," she complained.

"Sleep in my bed, Nettie. I don't mind. I don't move around like you do. I probably won't sleep anyway."

"Why ever not? Anyone would think you'd sleep like a baby. After you just became betrothed to a fine handsome man." The sarcasm of her words hung in the air heavier than the perfume

"So that's it? You are jealous." Elise peered at her sister in the dim light. "Your turn will come sooner than you think. And I just hope you will be happy with the choice Papa makes for you." Elise fought back emotions that had been building all evening.

"If he arranges a match for me like he did between you and Derrick Homes I would get down on my knees and thank the Almighty." Nettie sat on the edge of her cot, punching her pillow into some softness. The cot creaked and collapsed and she went sprawling across the floor. She groaned loudly.

Elise giggled, too exhausted to reprimand her. "Nettie, don't be dazzled by Derrick's looks and wealth. He's not the nice person you want to believe." She began rearranging the covers on the floor to make a comfortable bed for both of them. "Please don't blame me, Nettie. I can't help what Papa does. I wish I could run away and hide but I can't. I know if I left I could never come home," she said dismally. "I couldn't bear it."

After a few moments, Nettie's breathing grew soft and even, and Elise lay back staring at the patterns on the ceiling created by the lanterns along the driveway and the leaves in the trees near the windows. The sounds of crickets filled the night. The brief encounter with Trevor held no comfort for her except for the moment when he actually seemed concerned. He believed she wanted power and wealth. Had it been so long ago that they were children with the same young dreams?

The moon came out from behind a cloud and flooded the room with light. It was like an omen lighting her life. Suddenly, for the first time that evening, everything became clear, and she realized Who was still in charge of her life. She prayed the prayer she had often said since she had returned home from school. She knew her faith was being tested and she vowed to remain steadfast. Soon the summer sounds lulled her. Only Nettie's fitful tossing and turning kept her from a restful sleep.

eight

"Please, Father," Justin pleaded. "I have never asked you for anything since I came here, but I am asking now."

Wilhelm rolled his eyes and stroked his beard. "That's not entirely correct. I seem to recall horses, saddles, even an automobile, though that request was denied on the basis of absurdity. You surely haven't earned anything as big as a house, Justin."

Inger wrung her hands and looked back and forth between the two men. Theirs had never been a flowing camaraderie. Justin clearly resented his frugal stepfather's wealth and power. Wilhelm, on the other hand, wanted from his stepson at least a passable interest in his business and some assistance in handling the estate. Justin's only interest was in gardening and, while the grounds flourished, the father-son relationship did not.

The rest of the family, assembled around the dinner table, watched in awkward silence. Even their guest, Derrick Homes, squirmed uncomfortably.

Undaunted, Justin continued. "If I must get to my knees and beg, I will do it." He knelt down by Wilhelm's chair and bowed his head as though waiting for a blessing.

"This is not the time, nor the place, Justin," his father said, looking around the table for support from the family. When none was forthcoming, he tugged at Justin to get up and said, "A house is a sizable matter, one not to be discussed over the dinner table."

Thick cords stood out at Justin's temples. He sent pleading glances to his mother, but she only shrugged, as though leaving the argument's outcome to the fates.

Justin took a deep breath. "All right, Papa." He rarely resorted to the pet name used by his stepsisters, but now he chose to do so. "I did not want to divulge my secret until I was certain. But since you are unwilling to grant my request, I see I must tell you why I am forced to resort to begging. I will need a house for my bride. Within a year I will take a wife." He watched the reactions on the faces of the others around the table, and his face relaxed into a smug smile. "How would you like a brood of grandchildren? I think you'd prefer them at a safe distance, wouldn't you? Would you really want them sharing the Traum with you?"

Wilhelm had been sipping beer, but now he choked and coughed, spraying a fine foam across his vest. Inger leaned forward with her mouth hanging open. The girls sat in stunned silence, but Derrick could not conceal his amusement.

"How can that be?" Inger demanded of her son. "We have never seen you in the company of a young woman except for your sisters."

"True, Mamma." Justin leaned away from his mother's flailing arms. "I have had my eye on someone in particular and when the time is right I will ask for her hand and only then shall I tell you her name."

"But you should go courting," Inger chided. "No girl wants to be told she is to be a wife at the last minute. Maybe she will not have you or maybe she has already been spoken for." Her blue eyes flashed and her mouth pursed.

"There is not one who would refuse such a fine

marriage, Inger." Wilhelm jumped to his feet and put a protective arm around Justin. "Don't push the boy. When the time is right he will tell us." He was now decided. "We will have some house plans drawn up. In the meantime, I will speak to Randall about taking you into the transportation business. Perhaps you will find it more to your taste than silk, eh?" He poked playfully at Justin's ribs.

"It is more than I had hoped for, Father. However, before I take a position in the company, I want to make sure the house is well under way. I think my work with trains best be delayed a few months."

"Construction can begin without you as an overseer," Wilhelm protested.

"But, Papa," Justin answered quickly. "I want everything to be perfect for my new bride and for your grandchildren. I want this home to be built with all native materials. There is slate and marble and fine wood right on our doorstep to rival the finest in Europe. It will also cut the costs and I, personally, will see to it that there is no extravagance in construction. Then, and only then, will I feel free to join my future brother-in-law in the railroad business."

"All right, Justin, we have an agreement—but believe that I will hold you to every word." The two men shook hands and everyone at the table relaxed.

Elise tried to ignore the fact that she was seated next to Derrick, who was engaged in deep conversation with her sister. Candlelight played provocatively with Nettie's soft blond hair and gave sparkle to her large eyes. Derrick's gaze never left her face except to pass the steaming bowls of food, the heavy German dishes that Inger insisted on serving every Sunday evening for the family dinner.

Elise felt her father's glare from the head of the table.

She tried to initiate conversation with Derrick, but Nettie kept up a running stream of idle chatter, flirting with him to the point that Elise was embarrassed for her sister. At last Elise gave up and sat back quietly, picking at her food. Wilhelm tried in vain to speak to Derrick about the railroad but the subject seemed to bore his future son-in-law. Finally, Elise excused herself from the table, saying that she was feeling ill. The men made halfhearted attempts to rise, but Nettie held up her hand.

"Poor dear," she said, "she hasn't felt well all day. Probably coming down with the summer complaint."

Elise headed straight for the front door and inhaled deeply of the night air, relieved to be out of the house. The coolness of the evening and the sounds of the light breeze rustling through the trees brought her calm. She had become more determined than ever to find some way out of the marriage. She and Derrick seemed to have the same opinion of each other and they would only have an impossible life together.

She wandered down the path below the terrace, knowing it from memory. The light from the house illuminated the benches and small shrubs. She took a seat and her dark silk dress blended with the shadows. Her breath caught at the thoughts she allowed herself to entertain. Betrothed to one man and thinking of another. She reminded herself of her promise to her father and her heart was heavy. She thought of all the things she would say to her mother, had she been alive. She would tell her of giving up her dreams, of wanting more from life than a husband who was destined to run into the arms of other women. What of love, she nearly moaned aloud. She shivered with the change of the night air, the coming of the dampness.

Voices on the path alerted her of someone's coming. She

sat very still, protected by the shadows, waiting for them to pass. Ahead were the silhouettes of two people with their arms entwined. Something made her remain still.

Nettie's laughter floated through the night. In the light from the house, Elise could see that she was looking up into the eyes of her escort. After awhile, she leaned her head on his chest and both of them drifted into the shadows. Elise heard their steps hesitate, as though they might have stopped to embrace.

She waited until they moved on. Her dress had become damp and her back ached with tension. She ran quietly up the path toward the house.

When she reached the side porch, two men sat on the rockers while Nettie passed lemonade to them as she softly hummed. She saw that one of them was Trevor, and she wondered how long he had been there and why. Had he been the one with Nettie? Elise continued around to the front door, leaving Nettie to entertain Derrick and Trevor.

❧

"I can't imagine why you must associate with the town riffraff. It's unthinkable that you should want to renew old acquaintances after all these years, Elise. You are an educated woman now. It's below your station." Spittle flew from Wilhelm's mouth as he tried to make his point.

"Is that the way you feel about the people who work for you every day ... that they're riffraff?" Elise's mouth contorted in anger.

"That's entirely different. They are my employees and I am their superior."

"It never ends, does it? You never come down from that tower that lets you see over their heads. You never get to a level with any of them." Her eyes blazed.

"I work shoulder to shoulder with any man there," he

said stiffly. "Why don't we just send a draft to their charity and leave it to that. There's no need for you to personally attend their picnic." He was almost pleading now as the women lined up against him. Even Inger stood with her arms crossed, determination written in the lines of her face.

Nettie reminisced, "Mamma used to pack a large hamper of food and all day long we would play games and listen to the music. I'll never forget those times. You're such a snob, Papa." She moved closer to Elise in unconscious defense.

"I doubt that you remember the picnics, Nettie. You were much too young," Wilhelm argued.

"I do so remember them, one in particular. I fell into the pond and had to be taken home, but Mamma insisted we go right back to the games."

Elise stared at her sister, surprised that she had remembered. "Oh, yes, Papa. I remember Mamma's white picnic dress and sharing our food with everyone. After that she insisted on providing a table of pies and cakes for everyone."

"Nonsense," Wilhelm retorted. "It sounds like a story you concocted just to get everyone in the spirit."

Nettie stood on tiptoe and put her arms around her father's neck. "I don't really care what happened in the past. I only know I want to go to the picnic today. Besides, Sam Williams from the hardware store promised to take me for a ride in his father's new Pierce Arrow. I wouldn't miss that for all the tea in China."

She backed up as her father began shaking his finger in her face. "I forbid you to gad about in fast automobiles, young lady," he screeched at her. Turning his anger on Elise, he pointed his finger at her now, "I hold you responsible for your sister's behavior."

She retaliated, "I can't be with her every minute, Papa. No one is responsible for Nettie's behavior except Nettie."

"Here, here," Nettie applauded. "I must congratulate you, Lise, as being the first in the family to accept that vital bit of information." Her high-pitched nervous laughter, however, belied her apparent confidence.

Justin came into the room, shaking his head. "I'll take full responsibility for Nettie, Father," he volunteered.

Nettie turned to look steadily into his gray eyes. "If you think you will ride in the back seat when Sam comes to pick me up, you're very mistaken, Jus, dear." She paused a moment in thought. "If he arrives before I come downstairs, please be a dear and have him wait in the parlor." Nettie winked and ran to change her dress for the third time that morning.

"That child will be the ruination of this family." Wilhelm complained, wrinkling his nose as Inger served him tea with his breakfast.

"Ah, Nettie is what gives this family class," Justin observed. "You will have to admit life is dull when she's not around to push us into true living."

"Most brothers are not so solicitous to their younger sisters. In fact, they usually can't stand them." Elise observed.

"Nettie's different," he argued. "I probably won't mind when you get married and leave us, but not Nettie."

Elise ran to the window as a horn sounded from the driveway. Sam sat honking and honking for Nettie to come out. Their father's dark look creased his cheeks above the beard. Finally, Sam got out and came into the house. Soon he was seated at the dining room table, enduring Wilhelm's tirade of questions about his intentions and the speed of his automobile. Justin glared at him with frank envy.

Finally, Nettie came down the stairs, turning every head

as though she had planned it. The filmy white dress she wore brought back memories Wilhelm would have willingly forgotten. Elise too was caught in a moment of deja vu. The family sat quietly as the couple drove away. Even Inger sensed the dress had been Edwynna's and kept silent.

A few minutes later, Derrick arrived with a team of handsome horses and a runabout. Wilhem watched his eldest daughter leave for the picnic with much greater approval than he had watched Nettie.

The size of the runabout's seat forced Derrick and Elise to sit closely, though neither spoke until they reached the picnic grounds. There, shirtsleeved men lined up at the kegs donated by the local brewery. Their shouts and high spirits soon brought Elise out of her doldrums, and she took Derrick's arm to be escorted across the green.

ﻼ

The excessive heat of mid-summer slowed the relay games until at last the contestants sought shade under the large oaks that dotted the banks of the stream. Some of the men and women waded in the creek with trouser legs rolled to the knees and skirts hoisted indecently. On the banks, women protected themselves from the sun with parasols.

Justin whispered to Elise as he came to sit on her blanket, "Next time I want you for my partner, sister dear. I was teamed up with a chap who could barely walk, let alone run. Your physical ability must be at least as good as his." His eyes never stopped scanning the crowd.

"You wouldn't want me for a partner if Nettie were here." She watched his searching gaze. "What's the matter? Did she give you the slip?" She laughed softly, fanning herself with her handkerchief, envying the women who dared to get their feet wet. Derrick was off to get some lemonade.

Elise watched while his eyes also searched the crowd.

Trevor came toward Elise with a young girl holding onto his arm. Self-consciously, the girl dropped her hand and stood by awkwardly as casual greetings were exchanged.

Trevor smiled, though his friend did not. "Thank you, Elise, for sending food and blankets to Chessie Stone. I'm not sure I can pull her daughter through this illness but I'm sure your generosity helped. I'm sorry you had already retired the other evening when I came to thank you personally. I missed you."

As always Elise was drawn to his great dark eyes. "I wanted to go visit Chessie myself but. . .I had another commitment." She felt a weight settle on her soul, for she knew she had committed the sin of speaking an outright falsehood; she had had no other commitment, but her father had prevented her from going into town to visit Chessie and her sick daughter.

"No doubt you had to attend some social tea—or something equally as pressing." His expression changed, and his companion snickered; obviously, they had sensed she was not speaking the truth. "Thank you again, Miss Waller," Justin said cooly.

Hurt filled her eyes as he walked slowly toward the lake. She was still staring after him when Derrick nudged her elbow with the hand holding her drink.

"Bothers you, does he?"

"He mocks me now but when we were children he was my friend." Her cheeks were flushed and dark strands of hair clung to her neck.

"I've seen the way he looks at you," Derrick commented. "You are no longer children, Elise. You are to be my wife and you should act accordingly."

Justin joined them again, looking warm and flustered.

"It's a conspiracy. You know where Nettie is and won't tell me."

Elise suppressed a smile. "Nettie is a free spirit. She would never confide that sort of thing to me. . .not lately, anyway."

Her attention was diverted to the top of the hill where a group of young people had come over the rise. In the center of them Nettie stood out in her white dress and frilly parasol. Justin followed Elise's gaze and went quickly to join the swarm of young men around Nettie. Her hair had been brushed to a sheen and cascaded down her back. Her lips were a brighter shade of pink than usual, though the color from the cosmetic box didn't cheapen her appearance the way it did some girls. The heightened color simply accented the clarity of her skin and the whiteness of her dress.

"Where have you been, Nettie?" Justin fumed from the edge of the entourage.

She ignored her stepbrother but stopped to shake hands with Derrick. They talked for several minutes in low tones, and she smiled captivatingly at him, as though he were relating an amusing story. Elise watched his face lose its sullen look.

Elise knew then that Nettie had orchestrated the whole affair, from her debut on the hill to this very moment. She also realized that no one here was even likely to notice if she herself were to simply disappear.

The heat was oppressive. Derrick came back to Elise's side and slept on the blanket with his head on her lap. She became cramped and stiff. When he stirred for a moment and opened his eyes, she excused herself and asked Justin to take her and Nettie home. Then she set off in search of her sister. Though dusk had fallen, Nettie was still surrounded by admirers.

"We have a ride, Nettie." Elise ignored Derrick who had come to stand behind her.

"Just one more trip to the lake, Lise." In spite of the long day, Nettie still bubbled. "The lake is so beautiful in the moonlight. Please, Lise."

"Papa will be angry."

"You're an old stick in the mud," Nettie pouted.

Justin interceded. "I promised I would watch out for you, Nettie."

"But there are so many here to watch out for me. Run along, Jus. I'll only be a few minutes."

From the edge of the crowd Trevor stood alone, watching the arguing sisters. "I'll see her home," he called. "The lake is beautiful, you know. The loons can be heard for miles. And there are flares around it tonight so it's not as dark as you imagine."

"Very well, Nettie," Elise said reluctantly. "But promise you will be home soon."

Nettie had already attached herself to Trevor. They were gone before Elise had time to reconsider.

The villagers were using wagons to carry the picnickers home. They sat on the hay in the back, singing and laughing together. Elise and Justin joined them, sitting silently side by side.

The hay wagon stopped at the Traum, and she and Justin got off. For a few minutes they stood on the wide porch listening to the fading music as the wagon drove away. As they entered the foyer, Wilhelm's shouts greeted them from the library. They hesitated, and for an instant Justin and Elise were united with a common bond. They both had to face their father.

nine

Later that night, loud voices echoed from the foyer, bringing the family out of their bedrooms to peer over the balcony. Inger and Elise exchanged nervous glances as the accusations became louder. Justin's door was slightly ajar as though he were listening but not wanting to be seen. Wilhelm was the one shouting, while Nettie's responses were nearly as loud.

"I sent one of the servants to find you and you were no where to be found," he accused. "He even stopped hay wagons but no one knew your whereabouts." His face had a sickly pallor in the light of the chandelier. He was completely dressed, but his clothes were rumpled, as though he had lain down in them while waiting for Nettie's return.

Nettie backed against the wall, using its support to brace herself. Her face was whiter than her dress. Her eyes were so downcast that to those on the balcony above, they appeared to be closed.

"Have you nothing to say for yourself?" her father demanded. Then, as some sixth sense tugged at his mind, warning him of the presence of an audience, he peered up at the balcony. "What are all of you gaping at?" he screamed, jabbing his finger in the air. "Go back to your beds and be quick about it. This is between me and Annette."

No one moved or spoke. The silence was charged.

Nettie was shaking, and when she answered him this

93

time, her words were breathless, strung together. "We were down at the lake. . .it started out as a good time. Some of the boys had been drinking too much. . .but he said it was all right, he could handle it." She giggled hysterically. "There were lights around the lake but we kept bumping into an overturned rowboat, tree stumps. . .it seemed so funny at the time. Then a fight broke out and we walked in the other direction." Her speech was thready at first but as she spoke, she seemed to gain strength, and the volume of her voice increased.

"Who is this marvel of a man who leads you around a dark lake at midnight? I want to meet him."

"It doesn't matter who he was. He's not to blame. I made him take me there. It was so beautiful, Papa, with all the flares. It was like a fairy tale. We even sat on the dock and dangled our feet in the water."

At that point Elise gripped the banister and peered more closely at her sister. Had she been with Trevor all this time?

"It smacks of one of those dime novels your Aunt Marguerite used to read. Trash, trash, trash," he spat.

"I wasn't thinking of the time, Papa. We just sat and talked." She was crying now and her face was wet with tears.

"My God, girl, have you taken leave of your senses?" He paced as far as the dining room door, cheeks puffed out, grunting to himself. "All I know is when they found you, they said whoever you were with ran into the woods. Why isn't he man enough to come forward and face me?"

Elise saw Justin's door close softly. He played watchdog on them all, she thought. He was a poor excuse for a man, in her estimation. Each day she disliked him more.

"It's over, Papa. I won't be so thoughtless again," Nettie

pleaded. "I just want to lie down and sleep now." She sagged back against the wall, then snapped to attention, as though she had just thought of something. "I know the next question on your mind—and I can tell you nothing happened tonight to compromise me," she said defiantly. Elise thought her sister looked as though her words had cost her her last ounce of strength.

Wilhelm seemed infuriated by her declaration rather than reassured. His breathing grew fast, and then, without warning, he dealt her a blow that staggered her. She fell to her knees on the parquet floor.

Inger and Elise moaned in unison, as though they too felt Nettie's pain. They started down the steps, but Wilhelm's hand raised, forbidding their interference.

"You'll be sorry for that," Nettie shrieked, holding her cheek and wiping blood from her lips.

"Watch what you say, young lady. Thank heavens you will soon be back in school. The head mistress will be informed that you are to have no privileges. You will live like a nun." His raised hand was about to descend on her again.

Slowly and deliberately, Nettie got to her feet and faced him once more. Elise could read the loathing in her sister's face and in every line of her bent body. Elise held her hand to her mouth, knowing full well what Nettie was about to say. She prayed Nettie would not choose this time.

When Nettie spoke at last, her words were barely more than a hiss. Inger and Elise strained to hear as she said, "I was going to wait until the day I was to be sent back to school but I will tell you this now." She paused and her voice grew loud, "I am not returning to that dungeon you call a school. Nothing you could do to me would make me go back there. I hate everything about it. I hate the witches who dole out their prissy patience as though it was God's gift. Now I am going to bed." She started toward the stairs but he blocked her way.

"You ungrateful little wench. You are just like your mother. She was willful and spoiled, too. You will do exactly as I tell you as long as you continue to live under my roof." He lifted his arm to strike her again. His face contorted and he turned red. As he stood there staring, he mouthed empty words. Suddenly, his arms dropped weakly to his sides, and he slumped, as though his body's strength had deserted him.

Inger ran down the stairs and guided him toward his room. He stumbled on the stairs, pausing by Elise. "I hold you responsible for this madness tonight. I will deal with you at breakfast." He drew himself up and walked past her. Inger looked neither right nor left but firmly gripped her husband's arm.

Elise waited on the top of the stairs for her sister. Nettie moved as though she were in a trance, walking straight toward Elise as though she did not see her. Elise refused to step aside. She took Nettie's arm and drew her down to sit beside her on the top step.

"Must we go into this?" Nettie whispered. "I'm exhausted."

"I need an explanation," Elise said firmly. "You owe me that much. If I'm to take the blame in a few hours I have the right to the full story." She put her arm around her sister and began to massage her back.

Nettie had closed her eyes, but Elise knew she was listening. On the one hand she felt pity for her sister, but on the other, fury was rising within her. "Nettie, you promised me."

Her sister turned her face to Elise. Elise gasped at the size of the welt on Nettie's cheek, and her anger disappeared. The two sisters fell weeping into each other's arms.

At last Elise asked, "Was it Trevor you were with? I wondered if he really stayed, since he still had his companion to see home. What happened?"

Nettie began sobbing again. "The whole thing was a mistake. I should have listened to you. There was a fight. It was a disaster." She closed her eyes and shuddered, reliving the events of the evening. She buried her face into her hands. "I'm sorry I got you into this mess, Lise."

Elise pushed the hair from her sister's face. She felt grass intertwined among the strands, and she put it in her pocket, not wanting to think about how it might have come to be there. "Tell me what happened tonight, Nettie."

Nettie stood up abruptly, avoiding Elise's questioning eyes. "Nothing, absolutely nothing."

Elise rose beside her and looked evenly into her sister's eyes. "A long time ago we agreed not to keep secrets.

After some thought, Nettie answered, "We were children when we made that promise, Lise. It was before. . ."

Elise kept her firm grip on Nettie's arm. "Nothing has changed. We are still sisters. We need each other, perhaps even more than we did."

Nettie's eyes held a faraway stare. "I want to believe that."

"It's true, Nettie. No matter how bad things get I will always be here for you, and so will God, dear one. I know you think it is foolish to talk about your faith—but God hasn't given up on you, Nettie, though you may have given up on Him. We are His sheep, even though we all stray from His fold."

The younger girl gulped back a sob.

Elise's heart ached for her sister. "By morning Papa will have forgotten the whole incident," Elise said comfortingly, though she doubted he really would. "Go to bed now. Pretend to sleep past the breakfast bell. We will delay what we can."

Nettie nodded and went dutifully to her room.

When Elise closed her own door, she sat at her dressing table for a long time. She traced her reflection in the small mirror, going over her downturned mouth and large sad eyes. Trevor had loved her mother once and now he was completing the broken circle with Nettie. She wished it didn't hurt so much.

❧

In the weeks that followed, Elise busied herself with the needs of the town's people, immersing herself so deeply in their troubles that she had neither time nor energy left to worry about her own. Meanwhile, Nettie became withdrawn and quiet, eating very little, speaking seldom. Elise felt as though she and her sister were both changing into different people.

One night, Elise tossed and turned in her bed, trapped in a dream. Someone was coming for her in the night, she thought. Chessie Stone's daughter, still not completely well, must have taken a turn for the worse. Elise tried to tell herself she was dreaming, but the sense of urgency still persisted. She felt pulled, but she was so tired, and her arms and legs would not obey her commands.

Outside her door, footsteps sounded, just like the dream. Elise roused, sure they would stop at her door to call her to some action. She sat up and felt the perspiration around her neck. No one came, though, and the running footsteps stopped.

Sleep claimed her again. Finally, waking to the bright glaring sunlight, she sat up and peered at the small china clock on the dresser. She rubbed her eyes to make sure she was seeing correctly. Her first thought was that she must go see Chessie and her daughter as soon as she could, for her dream's sense of urgency still lingered in her mind.

She dressed casually and was tiptoeing down the hall when she heard loud voices coming from downstairs. She stood still, listening.

Her father's voice boomed through the hallway in its usual timbre. Another man's voice was more subdued. Elise sensed a feeling of urgency in their voices, and she felt alarmed. The constant bickering between her father and Nettie in the weeks since the picnic, the undertow between everyone, Nettie's withdrawal from living—all of it had been awful. Now, though, she sensed that something even more serious had occurred.

For some strange reason the hair stood on the back of her neck. She ran halfway down the stairs.

"It's about time you were up, Elise," Inger scolded from the foyer.

"You know I've hardly slept in days, Inger. I've been spending all my time trying to find a house for that poor unfortunate family that had the fire."

Wilhelm glared at her, "What do you mean coming down here so late in the day?" He glanced nervously from her to the hired man who stood at the door. There was a look of secrecy between the two men. Finally, Wilhelm prodded the man to leave. He shifted his hat from one hand to the other and backed out of the door.

"Is there trouble at the mill?" Vaguely, she remembered seeing the man before. "Is there anything wrong?"

"We will talk in the library," he commanded. "It will be all over Schiffley that you came downstairs in the middle of the day."

Wide-eyed, Elise turned to Inger. "Tell me what it is? I know something has happened." She stared at their somber faces, recognizing for the first time that Inger had been crying. Her head began to swim.

"Your sister is not here," Inger sniffed. "She is gone."

Elise flew down the stairs to her father's side. She held onto him as he was about to open the front door. "Where is she, Papa? Do you know?" Her large dark eyes pleaded with him as her hands grasped his arm.

"She didn't come home last night. She never comes home on time," he complained. He sounded drained and tired.

Elise sat weakly in the bottom step. "It's not like Nettie to go off alone." She was remembering how Nettie had changed since the night of the picnic. A skin-prickling guilt crept over Elise. She should have recognized that Nettie was deeply troubled.

"You may as well hear it all," said Wilhelm.

Her eyes met his, flinching at the awful sorrow she saw there. Wilhelm leaned close as though he wanted to reach out and touch her. When he drew back she knew the moment of impulse had passed.

"A carriage has been found that she must have used to leave the grounds. Though how she could have managed to hitch up the team alone I can't understand. They were found down by the lake on the road to Schiffley."

Elise's gaze flew between Inger and her father. "You think she's dead, don't you?" she demanded. "You are talking like Nettie no longer exists rather than being missing for a few hours. Well, I don't believe it for a minute." She shook her head vehemently, not taking her eyes from his face. "How can you think such a terrible thing?" she accused.

"Even if she has left this house on her own free will she is as good as dead."

"You can't mean that." Her face went pale.

"I mean it."

"Either way, in death or life, you are dismissing her as dead," she screamed and beat her fists on his broad chest.

Coldly, he stared down at her, holding her flailing arms at her sides. "Either way," he repeated, "my daughter is dead to me. You can see the panic she has caused everyone. Inger is sick with grief, you and I are at each other's throats as we have never been, even over Derrick. Poor Justin hasn't even been told yet. If this is a trick, it is a cruel one. She is better off dead."

"Please, Papa, let me go and look for her before you make this awful declaration."

"Men have been searching all night."

"But she may have met with an accident," she protested. As she spoke, servants were carrying hat boxes and chests from Nettie's room. "Don't you dare empty her room. Take her things into mine." Tears streamed down her face as she glared at her father.

He turned on his heel and slammed out of the front door.

Elise tore it open and screamed behind him, "You will change your mind someday and I'll be here to remind you. You couldn't keep her a prisoner forever. You love Nettie, I know you do. You will go after your lost sheep, I know you will." She stood on the porch looking after him. Her shawl had fallen from her shoulders and her gray dress swirled in the stiff wind.

Wilhelm turned to face her. "And what of you, Elise?

Are you a prisoner, too?" Then he hurried off to the stables.

When she finally closed the door behind her, she fully expected to find Inger and the servants clustered around. Instead the hall was empty. She wrapped the shawl tightly to her body. The house echoed of things past and of things unknown and terrifying. She felt like a child walking into a strange new place.

She wandered into the parlor where it was being redecorated in anticipation of a wedding. The piano was covered with a gaudy piece of chintz in Inger's Germanic taste. There was no music in the house. With Nettie gone, there would never be music again.

Impulsively, she drew a sheaf of paper from the mahogany writing desk and dipped the pen into the inkstand. She hesitated only a moment and then her fingers flew across the white paper. At last she reached for the blotter, and pressed hot wax to the seal. A servant was summoned to post the letter.

Perhaps Aunt Marguerite would have some news of Nettie. Of one thing Elise was sure: her sister was alive. She tried to cast off the feeling of deep depression as she began talking to God.

ten

The evening of Nettie's disappearance Wilhelm waited in the library for Justin to come home. He hadn't seen the necessity of sending a message to the house work site. Nothing would be changed except Justin's frame of mind. But in the meantime, Wilhelm fumed and paced. Several times he was heard to moan aloud as the servants tiptoed around outside of the library.

The loudness of his voice had not diminished with age. Nor had the permanent scowl on his face that had carved deep lines into his cheeks, lines that no longer disappeared when he laughed. For Wilhelm never laughed and he smiled for only brief moments. He found life too demanding for joviality. He was a practical man. Laughter soon died away, he reasoned, and life had to be met on its own serious terms. Besides, laughter caused men to view the world through rose-colored glasses and make sorry decisions which often confined them to years of drudgery. He had vowed, while still a boy, to meet challenge and opportunity with a clear head, to make the most of his life. Had he been a man of religious conviction he would have adhered strictly to the teachings of the Bible. Instead, however, he had created his own creed, and he followed strictly its own unyielding tenets.

The click of the front door brought Wilhelm into the hall-way. He glared when he saw Justin grinding grit into the polished floor with his mud-caked boots. Through clenched teeth, Wilhelm shouted, "Go outside and remove your boots."

Exhausted from a long session with the builder, Justin was about to argue, but the look on his father's face made him stop. He stepped back through the front door and took his boots off outside, then quickly returned.

"Why don't we sit in the parlor, Father?" He stood barefoot in front of Wilhelm. "I'd like a glass of wine before I bathe."

Wilhelm did not move. "I have something to say to you— a matter of the utmost importance."

Despite the grimness on his father's face, Justin was amused. "Apparently, whatever you have to tell me is not so important, however, as keeping the floors clean."

"You smile," his father mumbled, steering him to the library, "because you don't know yet what has happened." He stared at Justin for a moment and then barked, "Your sister, Annette, has disappeared. . .we do not know her whereabouts at present. Mark my word, though, I shall have all the information shortly."

Justin stood absolutely rigid. His face went ashen and his jaws worked. "Oh no, oh no. My Nettie," he half moaned. The strangeness of the sound brought Inger from the dining room where she had been waiting for him to come home.

"Sit down, Justin," she commanded. "You look like a ghost, *liebchen*." She stroked his hair back from his drawn face, at the same time guiding him to the leather couch. He pushed her away. Tears streamed down his face.

"Get a hold on yourself," Wilhelm boomed. "Stop this nonsense. I know you adored Annette but she has made her own bed and there's nothing we can do about it." He refused to admit that some harm could have come to his daughter. Her willfulness gave him little doubt that she had left the house because of some scheme of her own, influenced by some person who had taken advantage of her impetuous nature.

Justin struggled to regain some composure. "How do you know she has run away? Did she leave a note?" His hands clenched.

"There was no note, but knowing Annette like I do, that is the only possible reason."

Inger sank into the leather couch she had intended for Justin. The leather squeaked and expelled air from the cushions as she sat heavily in it. Her eyes glared at her husband. He had no sympathy for her son.

Finally, Justin fell into his mother's arms. "How could she do this to me, *Mutte*? Why would she run off without talking to me first?" He sobbed openly, no longer trying to control himself. "We were more than friends," he wailed.

She rocked him in her great bosom, hushing him as though he were a child. "Hush, Justin dear. She may have gone back to school to get away from all the strain at home. I know she told her father she wasn't going back, but it is just like a young one to change her mind." She wiped the tears from her eyes and became practical. "Now do what your Papa says and change your clothes. I will set a plate for you and we will sit together while we eat."

"No food," Justin said as though the sight of it would make him sick. Hurriedly, he left the room. Inger watched her son go up the stairs, her face a mask of unspoken fear. When she turned to Wilhelm, though, she was smiling. "It will be all right, you will see."

Early in the evening of the second day, a chill of fear rippled through the Traum; one of the local boys found some discarded clothing under a bush near the lake. The skirt was not positively identified as Nettie's, but Wilhelm insisted the lake be dredged. The search went on far into the night. Great fires were lighted, and village boys were paid a penny each time they dived. By midnight, no body was found, and the boys refused to dive into the murky waters again.

Inger and Elise kept vigil on the bank, while Justin dived countless times into the water until he became too exhausted to do anything but huddle shivering on the shore, barking orders to others. Elise finally coaxed him to the carriage so that he could return to the house for a hot bath and some food.

He shivered in a blanket as she drove him home. "You never were a good sister to her, you know," he accused.

"She's not dead, Justin," she answered tightly. "Tonight was a waste of everyone's time. If I believed in such things, I would have been willing to wager she wouldn't be found. I know Nettie better than any of you, no matter what you think of me. She may have run away but she would never kill herself. She was raised in a Christian home, in spite of my father's denial. She knows what a sin it would be to take her own life. And besides, despite all the troubles we've had lately, Nettie still loves living too much to wish an end to everything."

"Someone could have killed her, did you ever think of that?" His mouth was a tight oval around his chattering teeth.

"I guess it is possible—but I know in my heart Nettie is alive. Have the faith of the mustard seed. No matter how small a kernel of faith we have left inside us, from it life

can grow. Nettie will be found." She put her hand out to
detain him as he got out of the buggy. "Justin, you are her
brother and she loves you—but it didn't stop her from leaving. She left me, too, though she and I have a bond between us that few sisters have. We must not blame each
other now. We need. . .each other." She was about to put
her arm around his shoulder, but he bounded from the carriage without a backward glance.

≈

From that moment Justin changed dramatically. His trans-
formation was closely observed by his mother if no one
else. Inger spent hours behind curtained windows, watching him come and go. She saw him return from his new
house, disheveled and gaunt, wearing the same clothing
for days on end. His eyes deepened in his head and a stubble
of beard grew on his chin. On one occasion, when he had
been gone for three days, one of the servants refused to
admit him to the front door. The maid who sent him to the
kitchen door, mistaking him for a beggar, was promptly
fired, but Inger knew the mistake was an understandable
one.

The work on his house came to a stop, too. Part of the
roof gaped in the crisp autumn air, and leaves swirled down
into the unfinished rooms. Justin had apparently lost interest in the new house. Inger wondered if he had abandoned
his plans to marry.

Early one morning when Wilhelm had gone to the mill,
Inger sat at the dining room table with her hands clasped
around a cup, her eyes staring at the wallpaper. Her hair,
usually neatly coiled, hung in thin strands over her ears.
Alerted by a sound at the front door, she hurried to the
window to look out.

Justin walked steadily in the direction of his house. Inger's pulse quickened when she saw the determination in his stride. Hoping he had renewed his interest in the new house, she grabbed a shawl from the hall closet and started after him, following clumsily across the wet grass. As she drew nearer to him, she recognized a tired doggedness to his gait, as though he had set himself one more task before he rested. He approached the front of the new house, and then he paused. Leaning over, he picked up something from the ground. Inger's mouth fell open as she watched her son heave a rock through the shining new front window.

She heard the tinkle of shattering glass, and she flinched as though she had been struck by the rock herself. Her shawl fell from her shoulders as her hands covered her face. An icy fear gripped her heart as she saw Justin disappear into the woods.

She was forced to admit at last that in the weeks since Annette's disappearance, her son had deteriorated to the point where she no longer knew what he was thinking; she could no longer credit her fears to her imagination, for in her heart, she knew imagination to be one of the many qualities she lacked. Inger had never been able to see anything except cold reality. She was deathly afraid of the reality which confronted her now.

ও

Elise was still trying to shake off her vague suspicions about Nettie and Trevor as she rode to Chessie Stone's cottage early one morning. As she had so many times before, she replayed the events of the last weeks again in her mind.

Nettie had been outrageously flirtatious at the picnic, Elise remembered. And Nettie had come home late after

Trevor had offered to look after her. Could he know something about her disappearance? Elise's thoughts were as unsettled as the dust that swirled around her as she guided her horse up the lane.

Wind had roamed the valley for several days, but it brought no relief to the dry autumn. Through the night, she had been disturbed by the sounds of dry leaves on her windowpane. She had drifted into a fitful sleep toward morning, only to be awakened by a messenger saying that Chessie's child had had a relapse; that Dr. Neavitt was on his rounds to the other side of the county and Dr. Lucas was delivering a baby—could Elise please come? Elise had struggled out of bed and hurried to the stables. Now, she struggled to shake away the sleep that still clouded her thoughts.

At last she saw the small light that burned in Chessie's window, a pale gleam in the early morning gloom. Elise hurried from her horse and knocked at the door. The woman who answered was barely more than a child herself, Elise thought. Chessie was frail and unkempt, her dress soiled, and her hair uncombed and knotted.

The cottage consisted of a single room with the barest of necessities. A small bed sat near the stone fireplace with the child lying on it. Even in the dimness, Elise could tell that the cottage was as untidy as the first time she had visited.

She dismissed any worries about cleanliness, however, when she saw Myra, her dark eyes shining unnaturally in her small face. Frequent bouts of coughing echoed through the room, and Elise saw that the child was now so weak she could not sit up. When the coughing ceased, the little girl fell asleep almost immediately, only to be awakened when the next paroxysm seized her.

Elise shivered, for the faint embers on the hearth did little to relieve the dampness in the house. "Has Dr. Lucas visited you yet this week, Chessie?"

Chessie shook her head. "The bottle of medicine is gone that he brought last week." She produced an empty bottle from under the bed.

"Have you eaten the food I sent?"

"We finished it yesterday. My brother and his family had some, too." Chessie grinned sheepishly. Then her face contorted. "She's gonna die, ain't she, Miss Waller?" She rocked on her heels and began to cry hysterically. "The Bible says the sins of the parents are visited on the children. I guess I done sinned when I had Myra single, without no husband." She lay down and cried and tore at her clothing.

"Hush, Chessie, we are all sinners in one way or another, but Jesus forgives each and every one of us. It gives us the strength for what we must endure in this life. Knowing He loves us and will take us home in the end makes our troubles here more bearable. You must be at peace knowing that, too. God loves you, Chessie." Elise stroked the coarse hair until the sobbing stopped.

A small squat man came into the cabin, the man from the next farm who had brought Chessie's plea for help to Elise. "Anything I can do to help, Miss Waller?" he asked.

Elise's mind began to race. "Please, take my horse and tell Dr. Lucas to come as soon as he is able. I pray the baby he is delivering will be born soon. Then stop at the kitchen door of the Traum and give them my note. They will send food with you, but, please, give my message to the doctor first," she begged.

The man looked none too happy to have his offer of help taken so literally, but nevertheless he grudgingly mounted the horse and set off at a leisurely pace.

"Be quick about it, please," Elise called after him. "I know that horse can go faster. And come right back," she urged.

Daylight was beginning to break as he rode off. Elise and Chessie took turns putting cool cloths to the child's head and holding her when she cried. Then they began cleaning the cottage. They discarded old straw from the bed and brought in new. They aired the house and washed the covers and hung them on the bushes outside. The sun-dried bedding and fresh hay gave a clean smell to the cottage.

As the day wore by and evening approached, Elise fought down the notion that the farmer was not coming back. Finally, after hours of waiting, they heard the horse in the lane. At his one slow pace, the farmer dismounted and handed Elise the hamper of food. He stood, waiting for some of it himself. When he had brought wood for the fire, she permitted him and Chessie to eat.

The farmer finished his last bite and pushed back from the table, saying, "Doc couldn't get away yet, but he sent this." He handed her a small bottle of medicine from his trouser pocket.

"Why didn't you give it to me right away?" Elise snatched at it. She thought of the times she had stood watching the child turn red and then blue as she coughed, while Elise held her own breath until rhythmic breathing returned.

"I guess I forgot. Doc was having his hands full—that woman he's with is having twins. He'll come as soon as he can."

"Thank you. Now go home to your family. There's

nothing more we can do but wait." She patted him on the shoulder, then wrapped some bread and meat in a cloth napkin and handed it to him to take along.

Around midnight, Myra had such a violent episode of coughing it brought both women to their feet. Then, amazingly, the child got out of bed and began dancing around. Chessie was elated and held her and cried with relief. Elise, however, was alarmed by Myra's flushed face. She touched the child, wincing when she felt the fever's burning heat. The coughing started again and rattled through the child's chest. In only a few minutes, she became lethargic again and slept once more, only to be awakened a few moments later by another bout of coughing.

When the racking cough reached a crescendo, Elise slapped her on her back. "Stop it, stop it!" she cried. "You have to live." She didn't know how long she pounded the little girl's back, but finally the coughing stopped and the child slept quietly. Chessie had been dozing, but she sat up now, awakened by the silence.

"Is she dead?" she asked timidly.

"No," Elise answered, "I think she's breathing easier. Come and see."

Chessie looked down at her daughter, then touched her face gently. "She is better, Miss Waller. She's cooler, too. Oh my God, it's a miracle. You done a miracle."

They cried in each other's arms. Then Elise arose and took some food from the basket; as she ate, she realized this was the first food she had had since she had eaten supper two nights before.

Trevor stood at the door as she sat sipping a cup of tea. "Everything seems under control here," he observed.

Elise stood up self-consciously. She smoothed her hair

and blushed slightly, while Chessie flew to Trevor and wrapped her arms around him. "She saved my baby. She stayed with us and she hit my little girl's back over and over. Miss Waller worked a miracle as sure as God is in His heaven." She bubbled over with words of praise for Elise.

"I'm sure it had more to do with the medicine you sent, Dr. Lucas, than anything I did."

"You are far too modest, Miss Waller. I couldn't have done any better myself. When you pounded on her back, you released the secretions in her lungs. It probably saved her life."

For the first time since she came home from boarding school, she saw admiration in his eyes. She could not tear her eyes away from his, feeling as though she had been thirsting and now at last could drink deeply.

"I'm sorry to hear about your sister. I wish I could tell you—" He broke off mid-sentence and began talking to Chessie and examining Myra.

"Will you come outside with me? I would have a word with you," he asked Elise when he had finished.

She followed him into the sunlight, pleased to be finally in his good graces. Their new relationship was still strained, but her heart pounded as she looked up at him.

"I owe you an apology, Elise. I understand you found a home for the family burned out in the fire. And here you are saving a child's life. I couldn't have done more myself. I thank you. My people thank you. Whatever your motives, you have given great service."

"Apology accepted, Trevor. I have no motives, as you put it. I only want to help those less fortunate than myself. Please believe me." She added, "Not everything is as it seems. Sometimes we are forced into situations not of our choosing." She longed to tell him of her commitment to her father and the engagement she detested, but something held her back.

"I wish I could tell you what you want to hear about Nettie." Trevor frowned and withdrew a step from her. "Mr. Homes should be able to console you in your loss."

She longed to deny her betrothal to Derrick, but the words faltered in her throat. "He has been very understanding," she admitted. "But nothing can take the place of a sister."

"You have everything to help you through your ordeal—friends, family, and your faith in God. Someday Nettie may come back to you and your world will be good again. In the meantime, I hope your wedding will be the grand occasion it is expected to be."

Every fiber in her body cried out to deny his words. "Everyone is too upset about Nettie's disappearance to think of a wedding."

Trevor shook his head. "I wasn't a part of the search for her—I feel that I owe you an explanation. However—" He shook his head again, apparently unable to continue.

A heavy silence fell between them. "I have always wondered what happened the night of the picnic," she said at last, reluctant to bring up the subject since their relationship had improved. "You promised to look out for her."

Trevor started to answer, but a carriage came racing up the road and stopped in front of them. Derrick jumped out and caught Elise's hand. "I've been all over the valley looking for you, Elise. It's time you came home where you belong. It's not fitting for you to spend so much time away from your obligations. Once we are married, this nonsense will stop. No wife of mine will spend the night in a hovel like this." He took her roughly by the arm and pushed her toward the carriage.

Trevor stood between Elise and the carriage. He was a head taller than Derrick, Elise noticed, and more muscular, and his presence gave her the courage to pull back against Derrick's grip on her hand. "This agreement that I am to do God's work is between my father and me. It has nothing to do with you, Derrick," she protested. "Besides, I am a long way from becoming your wife." Anger flashed in her dark eyes.

Derrick tried to ignore Trevor's unmoving presence. "I have an appointment with your father, my dear, and together we are going to inform him you have changed your mind and have decided to set the date of the wedding for next week."

Elise laughed. "Papa has granted me until my eighteenth birthday. It is an agreement between us and has nothing to do with you."

She glanced at Trevor and saw the astonishment in his eyes. The open disagreement with Derrick had done more to inform Trevor of her predicament than any words she could have spoken. She was glad for the look on his face. Silently, she thanked God for providing her with a way to tell Trevor she was being forced into the marriage. Satisfied that her two days had ended in total success, both for the child and herself, she got into the carriage without further argument and permitted Derrick to drive her home.

eleven

As was his custom, Wilhelm read Aunt Marguerite's letter aloud at the dinner table. At his side, Inger listened lethargically as he read in the sing-song voice he reserved for his sister-in-law's letters. First his voice was a high-pitched whine, then low and almost giggly. Often he peered over his spectacles to make sure all were attentive. Elise smiled, though tears sprang to her eyes because her father didn't have his usual audience to spur him on; Nettie had always goaded him until they all laughed with tears streaming down their cheeks. At one point, halfway into the second page, her father must have been struck with the same memory, for he paused for a long moment, and then his voice turned normal and subdued. His words droned on until the third page—and then abruptly he fell silent. He read the remainder of the letter to himself, his hands shaking as they held the pages.

Elise leaned forward, sensing something important in the unspoken silence. "Please read the rest." Her hunch had been right after all, she thought; Nettie must be with Marguerite.

"Go on, Father," Justin urged.

Even Inger sat straighter in her chair.

Wilhelm blinked as though there was something in his eye. He wiped his moist lips with the napkin, though no food had been in his mouth yet. With trembling hands, he picked up the letter again and with a great sigh, began to

116

read. "Your daughter Annette has been a guest in my house for several weeks now. Though I know she wouldn't approve, I write on her behalf." He stopped reading and looked helplessly from one to the other. A serving girl paused over a tray of food on the sideboard.

Elise gasped and sat back in relief. Nettie was safe and with Marguerite. Her mind flooded with questions, and tears poured down her cheeks. "Don't stop, Papa. I want to hear every bit," she begged.

Justin tried to snatch the letter, but his father pulled it away. "Yes, yes, we want to hear all there is," Justin cried. A tinge of color rose in his face.

"I think this is a private matter," Wilhelm said harshly.

"Not when it mentions Nettie," Elise protested. "We all want to know why she left home, though it is almost enough to know she is alive and safe."

"Please, Wilhelm," Inger reached out and put a hand on his arm. "We are all waiting for you to continue."

He swallowed with great effort, then took time to adjust his spectacles. His face had paled, accenting his graying beard and intense dark eyes. He cleared his throat for the third time. On this reading there was no mimicking the falsetto in Marguerite's voice. When he finished they sat in stunned silence.

"She doesn't believe there is a place for her in the Traum. How lonely she must feel. And Aunt Marguerite insists it is because she doesn't want to return to school. I wish I could believe that was all that was to it," Elise thought out loud.

"Ask her to come home, Father. She needs us," Justin declared, jumping to his feet. He began pacing the length of the dining room.

"Does she indeed?" Wilhelm stood up suddenly, spilling

a goblet of red wine across the white tablecloth. He gasped
and his face turned pale as he stared at the wine-soaked
cloth. "See? It is a sign that blood will be spilled. A curse
has come to this house." He stared at Justin who had
stopped his pacing and stood perfectly still.

Elise felt faint. She didn't believe in curses but she could
see the effect it was having on her father. "Please, Papa,
ask her to come home," she choked.

"Yes," Justin whispered hoarsely.

"You? You?" He pointed to Elise, then Justin. "Why
should either of you speak for her? She has always been
your rival, Elise. And you, Justin. You don't know your
place in life. You build a house for a woman we have never
met. You let yourself smell like the stables. I will have
none of this talk from either of you."

Justin stormed out of the room with his father shrieking
after him, "I absolutely forbid her back in this house. Do
you hear me?" Wilhelm's arms and fists flailed the air.
The outer door slammed, and he slumped in his chair at
the head of the table, staring into space.

"He's right, you know," Elise took up where Justin had
left off, but more quietly. "Nettie needs you to hold out a
hand to her. She must be frightened at the thought of never
seeing her family again. She's so young, Papa."

"Then let her lean on Marguerite or her lover, if she has
one. What she did to cause us this grief is unforgivable."
His face was etched with pain.

Elise let a long, silent moment go by, and then she ven-
tured, "Papa, Nettie must find Aunt Marguerite tedious.
Please invite her for a visit, at least."

"No," he shouted so loudly it echoed through the house.
He wiped his mouth on his napkin again, folded it neatly,
and placed it on his empty plate. He looked from Elise to

Inger to make it perfectly clear he was addressing them both. "There will be absolutely no correspondence from this house. I forbid it. *Verboten!* Understood?" Then he marched quickly from the room.

When he had left, Inger went to the window that looked toward Justin's house. A small light gleamed in one of the rooms. Without a word or backward glance, she went to her room.

Elise remained at the table, toying with a fork. One of the serving girls started to clear the table and was startled to see her sitting there.

"Excuse me, Miss Elise. I didn't know you were still here. I will come back later."

"It's all right, Ruth," she said. Then she followed the maid to the kitchen. She stood pale and quiet until all noise ceased and the staff waited for her to speak.

"We have just learned that Miss Annette is ... is all right. She is visiting our Aunt Marguerite in Philadelphia. I am aware of your concern for her and I wanted to let you know she is safe." She left quickly to the soft applause of the staff.

Justin came into the house as she started up the stairs. They stopped and studied each other for a moment. Neither spoke. As she went upstairs, Elise was acutely aware that he was still watching her.

Once inside her room, she let loose the flood of pent up emotions. Her head ached and her stomach churned. In total despair she turned to God to share her burden. In the coolness of her room, a calmness filled her mind and body, and she stopped crying.

In her mind's eye, she focused on the pastel sheets of paper that had brought the message. Aunt Marguerite had hinted of being tired of playing nursemaid. Nettie must be an imposition in Marguerite's well-ordered house. Wilhelm had forbidden any contact with her, but logical reason began to replace Elise's first emotional outburst. She would have to find a way around her father's orders.

≈

Life soon settled back into its dull routine. Each Sunday Derrick called to take Elise to church. He arrived with flowers and candy as would any serious suitor, and Elise began to see a new side to him. He was obviously trying to abide by his part of the agreement and, when he chose to, he could be decent and charming. He even seemed willing to forget that they had started off on the wrong foot. His easy manner and attentiveness soon put to rest the fear that he was the brutish man she had first met. He no longer pressed her to set a new date for their wedding. Eventually, she had to admit she even liked him in some small way.

After church they often drove around the countryside in Derrick's automobile, sometimes using the sleigh when the roads were impassable. They went to the stream to see the hoarfrost on the trees along the banks. They used their time together to learn more about each other, sometimes telling their hopes and dreams for the future. Elise settled into an acceptance of her forthcoming marriage; she no longer loathed Derrick, though her heart still tugged elsewhere.

It had been weeks since the letter came about Nettie. Derrick had been told simply that Nettie was discovered to be visiting with a family member. On this particular Sunday, Elise longed to talk to someone about her sister. She decided to confide her frustrations to Derrick.

She regretted her decision, however, the moment the words left her mouth. "I wish there was a way around

Papa's ban to have contact with Nettie," she finished, and then blushed, noticing at once his silence and the grim expression on his face.

Unable to help herself once she had begun, she blurted, "Papa has disowned her. There's no one I can talk to about it. . .except Justin and Inger and they are both locked away in their own worlds." She gushed on, a flood of confidences out of control, "I don't know what to make of Justin, the poor boy, except that he adored Nettie. He was totally crushed that she didn't confide in him."

Derrick turned toward her then, and when she saw his expression, her gloved hands flew to her face. He stopped the sleigh just before they came to the Traum and took her hands in his. "I will always listen to you, Elise," he said gravely. "Tell me more. I would like to help."

The presence of his hands on hers was reassuring. She talked breathlessly, glad to have found a vent at last. "Everyone loves Nettie. I suppose that's the way it has always been. I accepted it a long time ago. . .that Papa loved her more than me. I don't know how he can just cut her off like that. . .like giving up his right arm." She sighed, looking over the countryside but not really seeing any of it. "I guess I don't miss her quite so much knowing she is all right. Still, she is hardly more than a baby."

"She's not a baby, Elise. You must stop thinking of her as one." A long silence grew between them. Finally he spoke again. "Your father is very much like mine, a stiff unyielding gentleman of the old school. Your father's feelings were probably very deeply hurt when Nettie ran away, but he wouldn't dream of showing it to anyone—so he acts like he doesn't care." He kissed her lightly on the cheek and they continued to the Traum. He held out his hand to help her from the sleigh.

"I know you are right, Derrick, but all I can see is his furor." She smiled, convinced by his kindness that she had been right after all to have confided in him. When he left her on the doorstep, she was filled with a feeling of relief that she had last expressed her confusion and fears.

Unfortunately, her feeling of peace was short-lived, for inside the house, she could hear her father and Justin in heated argument. She paused near the library door, trying to make sense of their accusations. At that moment the door burst open, and Justin slammed it behind him. Angry slashes of color streaked his cheeks. Wilhelm tore after him and glared at the sight of Elise. "What are you doing here?" he asked.

"Waiting for an audience with you," she smiled sweetly.

"Well, I don't want to discuss your sister, is that clear? It seems to be the only subject on everyone's mind these days. The subject is closed, once and for all." He kicked the lower step, almost knocking Elise down on his way to his room.

Elise hummed to herself. A plan was forming in her head. God had shown her the way.

෴

The house was heavily garlanded and decorated with paper mache bows and silver angels in lacy gowns. Greens cascaded from the upstairs balcony, spilling over into the dining room where giant topiaries with lacquered fruit and nuts stood on each side of the double doors. In the parlor a large fir tree was decorated with icy tinsel and handmade ornaments. Here and there a crocheted doily accented the white candles that gleamed on the tip of every branch.

When Elise stepped onto the balcony, she was greeted by the smell of gingerbread. She almost expected Nettie to come bounding from her room like when they were children. Elise tilted her head, trying hard to recapture the moments time had stolen. She peered into the empty hallway—but Nettie was never coming home again, and Elise's heart ached with heaviness.

Inger and Wilhelm joined her on the balcony to go downstairs together in their Christmas tradition. No mention was made of Justin. Even Wilhelm's Christmas greeting was missing. He made a pretense at joviality but his words sounded hollow.

"I'm glad you are joining us for breakfast this morning, *liebchen*," he said absently. "I wish you. . ." Elise could not bear the far-away look in his eyes or the way his speech trailed off mid-sentence.

She paused on the bottom step. "I'll be down in a minute." She retreated back to her room and leaned against the door, her breath coming in short catches. How could she face a day so steeped in memory? She longed to talk to Trevor about Nettie, knowing that she would find comfort in his quiet strength, but he seemed to be avoiding her.

She turned toward her mirror and smoothed a few strands of dark hair from her flushed face. Her hands were icy cold. She ran a brush through her hair and recognized the panic in the dark eyes that stared back. For a few minutes, she sat on her bed until she felt control returning.

At last she took a deep breath and opened the door to the hall. Memories crouched among the greens on the landing, but she ignored them. The sun streaked through the stained glass windows and cast a yellowish light. . .Nettie used to call it. . .But no, she would not pay attention to the memories that crowded her Christmas with Christmases past. She hurried to breakfast.

This was the one day of the year Wilhelm gave his workers off and so only a skeleton crew served breakfast and laid out a buffet for the rest of the day; then they were gone to their families.

After Elise had eaten, she slipped to the parlor where only four stockings hung at the fireplace. She unfolded Nettie's from her pocket and slipped her gift into it, watching as it slid to the toe. Alone in the room, she whispered, "This is my gift to you, Nettie. I haven't forgotten how much you love surprises. I know God is watching over you and He will see to it that we will meet again." She was startled by the tight hysterical quality in her voice. Going quickly to the tall Christmas tree, she plucked a silver ornament from its branches and tucked it into Nettie's stocking. "This is your favorite," she said of the ornate manger and Christ Child. Half whispering, half aloud she said, "I'm coming to see you, Nettie. I miss you so much." She closed her eyes and when she opened them the tree was ablaze with light. A servant had seen her standing there and came to light the candles. She thanked him and patted the folded stocking in her pocket.

Wilhelm came into the room and pleaded with her, "Come into the dining room so we can open our gifts, Elise. I'm sure there is a surprise for you."

"Not now, Papa. It's such a lovely morning I thought I would take a walk." She saw a pained look on his face as she ran to the hall closet for her cape. The wind was raw but she didn't mind it. The sight of the lighted tree was more than she could bear.

For a long time she walked and thought. When she returned to the house, she knew exactly what she would do.

twelve

The next morning, Elise went to breakfast early in an attempt to avoid her father. He was already there, however, looking curiously at her as she sat down opposite him. Justin came and grabbed a roll, then left again without a word of greeting.

This morning, Wilhelm took time for the pleasantries he usually dismissed. He rose until she sat. He made sure she was served before himself. He was amiably inclined to conversation. "I'm glad that boy is thinking of something worthwhile again," he said after Justin had come and gone. "Now he's even talking to Derrick about a position on the railroad. I suppose everything is shaping up after all. Almost everything, that is."

"Why do I have the feeling I am the 'almost everything'?" Elise asked, meeting her father's intent stare.

"The mill is at peak production, Elise. Derrick assures me we can double our production if we were to merge immediately. I know I gave you my word, daughter, but it is imperative that you do not postpone your marriage until your birthday." He sat back and waited, expecting her to agree.

"In all my life, Papa, you have always kept your promises. Good or bad, you kept your word. Why is this so different?"

"Because it can make or break my business." His nostrils flared and his voice rose. "As it is, I will have to let some of my workers go. The winter is a hard time to sell silk." His voice was mincing, his tones almost pitiful.

"That's not fair. You are making me responsible for employees losing their jobs. Really, Papa!" She slammed her cup on the saucer, spilling tea onto the tablecloth. Fury shone in her eyes.

Wilhelm softened his tone. "I have watched you and Derrick getting along famously. Why delay the wedding?"

She regarded him coolly. "I'm not backing down, though it's apparent you are." She tried to inject some enthusiasm in her voice. "I am going to the city today on the early train." She produced a list tucked in her shirtwaist. "It's high time I began shopping for some wedding clothes. I don't expect to be home until evening."

He was silent.

"Well, this is what you wanted," she accused.

"No need to take the train. One of the men can drive you to Allentown."

"I'm taking the train to Philadelphia," she answered and watched as he abruptly stopped chewing his roll.

"Aunt Marguerite just happens to live in Philadelphia." His voice was hard.

"Look at my list. Don't you think that's enough to keep me busy without my going visiting?" She avoided his eyes.

"Then let me send someone with you to carry your purchases," he insisted.

"What do men know of women's shopping? Whoever you sent would not understand why I would need to linger here or move on immediately somewhere else where nothing struck my fancy. We would be sure to drive each other to distraction. No, if I buy more than I can carry, I will have it delivered." She jammed her mouth full of food so she would have an excuse not to answer his next question.

At last he gave in. "The phaeton will be hitched and ready to take you to the station. If our depot were completed and the railroad brought to Schiffley, this whole arrangement would be much more practical, you know."

She nodded, not wanting to get onto the marriage subject again. When he left for the mill, she tingled with excitement as her carriage arrived at the door.

ใจ

Hours later when she arrived at last in Philadelphia, Elise went directly to a hat store and purchased a bonnet to wear with her spring suit. Then crossing the wide street between the comings and goings of automobile traffic, she bought a riding habit and decided on a colorful scarf for Inger. She had made impulsive choices at the suggestion of the sales clerk in the department store, because paramount in her mind was seeing Nettie. She didn't know what to expect from her or from Marguerite. Resentment or warmth, bitterness or joy, they could all be forthcoming from her visit. Her hands were icy cold, and the heavy coat and muff did little to ward off the chill that gripped her.

The cab drove slowly through the residential neighborhood, elegant houses beside more modest ones. She tried hard to remember Marguerites's house but was surprised when the cab stopped in front of a federal style brick building, small in comparison to its neighbors and set back behind a high wrought iron fence.

Standing on the front step, Elise assured herself she had done the right thing to come. She would ask her father's forgiveness later, and God's too for disobeying her father, but somehow she felt that God wanted her to be here. After all, she had felt all along that He had given her this idea.

She pulled the door bell a second time. This time, she heard someone coming from within the house. She took a deep breath and pulled herself up straight.

Marguerite answered the door wearing a common house dress, devoid of the fineries she always brought to the Traum. If she was surprised to see Elise, she didn't show it. "I wondered how long it would take one of you to come," she said with sarcasm in her voice, making no move to embrace her niece.

"If it were up to Papa no one would be here," Elise answered. "But I am here, Aunt Marguerite. May I come in?"

"Of course." She stepped back. "The maid is tending to Nettie. She has been depressed and very weak. She no longer wants to live." She hurried to add, "But she is young and healthy and I'm sure she will be all right. It was quite a shock to her when no one asked her to come home."

Elise studied the frail-looking woman. "It is most kind of you to offer your home to Nettie. I'm sure it is an imposition."

She followed her aunt up to Nettie's room, noticing the clutter in the rooms and the thin layer of dust on the furniture.

When Elise stepped through the bedroom door, the frail girl on the bed held her arms out to Elise and wept uncontrollably. Then they held each other in silence for a long time. Finally, Nettie lay back with a great sigh. She was pale and thin, and dark circles underlined her great blue eyes, emphasizing her small face.

"I never thought you would have to see me like this," she sobbed.

"Shh, dear Nettie. It will be all right. You will soon be

back to good health and laughing again. You are weak now. Soon you will be feeling like your old self." Elise's heart cried out to the girl on the bed, but she closed her eyes to the sight before her, unable to bear what she saw. Nettie's face had always been smiling, framed by childish curls. The girl on the bed had become a woman since they last met.

"How is Papa?" Nettle asked with longing in her eyes.

"As brash as ever," Elise answered thickly.

"I think Nettie will have to rest now," Marguerite said at the foot of the bed.

Elise had mixed feelings about leaving her sister so soon, but before she was out of the room, Nettie had fallen asleep.

When Elise and her aunt had gone downstairs for a cup of tea, she turned angrily to Marguerite. "She looks terrible. Why is she in such rundown condition? I don't understand."

In defense, Marguerite's temper flared as Elise had seen it do a hundred times. "It's not my fault the girl feels abandoned. She is so homesick she practically has to be spoon fed." Her voice melted and the pinched expression on her face faded. "Perhaps your coming will do some good."

"If only Papa could see her this way. I'm sure he would change his mind."

"I know how vile his temper can be and what an unyielding old fool he is."

Elise studied the small feisty woman, admiring her strength.

"You must know, of course, as contemptible as he is, I have always loved him," Marguerite admitted.

Elise's eyes grew wide. "That surprises me. All you have ever done is fight with him."

"I wanted him desperately after your mother died. When I came to look after you, I thought I had a chance, but he must have recognized how alike we are, he and I. When he went off to Germany and came back with that dull *hausfrau* I was crushed. I will never forgive him for that. Just like I never forgave him for what he did to your mother."

"What do you mean?" Elise's eyes grew large as she leaned forward.

"Oh, your mother's death was an accident pure and simple." She laughed lightly and for the first time put a hand on Elise's arm. "But he may have unwittingly had a hand in her death. They fought so violently. He was extremely jealous. It was a mistake to allow that French count in the Traum. He had followed your mother home from Europe just to decorate the house, he said. . .All the gossip that followed. . .it was just too much for Wilhelm, I'm afraid. He accused your mother, and they fought. One thing led to another, and. . .your mother ran from him, fleeing to the cliffs where she loved to sit and look over the land. She was upset, though, and the rocks were wet. She. . ." Marguerite fell silent, her eyes bitter.

Elise tried to remember the events Marguerite spoke of, but she could only do so through the eyes of a child. One thing that did stand out in her mind, however, was that her father had completely redecorated the house after her mother's death, stripping it completely of the French influence, all except the salon that her mother had personally decorated.

"You have given me much to think about, Aunt Marguerite. Perhaps I will have a new approach with my father." She got up and hugged her aunt. The embrace was returned. "There is one thing I have to ask you before

I go. It has long been on my mind. How is it that Nettie came to be here? Who helped her?" She leaned forward again, her lips parted in anticipation of the answer.

"Why, it was Dr. Lucas. I'm surprised you didn't know, Elise. They seemed so close I thought there might have been a romance," she giggled.

Elise sat back, shaken and thoughtful. She never got to speak to Nettie again that day. She had fallen into the most restful sleep since she stayed with Marguerite, and they chose not to disturb her.

All the way home on the train, Elise was accompanied by a feeling of impending doom. She felt betrayed by Trevor and her heart ached. He had had the opportunity to tell her about Nettie but did not, letting her go on frantically thinking the worst. Her mind clouded with dark thoughts.

He owed her nothing, after all; in fact, he was little more than an acquaintance. She yearned for their relationship to be much more, she admitted to herself, but he had told her to find her consolation with Derrick. Obviously, she meant nothing to him.

Her few parcels lay on the seat beside her, hardly enough to be the result of a day's shopping. She wanted desperately to tell her father how Nettie needed him, now more than ever. She reached into her reticule for a handkerchief, and her fingers touched the forgotten Christmas stocking neatly folded around the gift and ornament.

She dropped it as though she was repulsed by finding it there. Yesterday it had seemed so important, but tonight no prayer was in her heart. Her sense of betrayal and sadness loomed high between her and God, though she felt guilt for not turning to God in a time of need. In spite of herself, she mouthed the words, "Thou dost hold my eyelids from closing. I am so troubled that I cannot speak." Slowly, a sense of peace crept through her tired mind.

≈

The gas lights in the house were dim as Elise stood in the foyer, brushing snow from her hair and shoulders. From the shadows where he had stood waiting for her, Wilhelm spoke, seeming to read her mind, "I'm going to have the house wired for electricity next week. Justin has been wanting me to be the first in Schiffley to have it."

"You've been waiting for me to come home I see," she said cheerily, restraining herself from blurting the truth about the day. "I bought this wonderful hat to wear with my suit. I had a swatch of the material with me," she explained. She put on the hat at the hall mirror and fussed about the tilt of it, hating the large feather that floated above it. "It seems darker than usual in here, Papa."

"I told the servants not to light the chandelier since there was no one here but myself. Justin is at his house and Inger has taken to her bed with a cough."

Elise jammed the hat back into the box, knowing full well she would never wear it. Wilhelm continued to hover over her.

"What else did you buy, daughter?"

"I found a lovely riding habit. And I bought a scarf for Inger. She likes bright colors."

"Anything else?" he inquired.

"That was all I found on my first outing."

"Nothing for your trousseau?" he asked casually.

"Why the riding outfit, of course. Derrick knows I love to ride. In fact, he wants to buy me a horse for a wedding present." She wanted to scream. Her head ached with all the opposing thoughts bumping into one another.

"With all that time to spare you must have seen Marguerite."

"I saw her for a few minutes." She evaded his eyes.

He slapped his leg in triumph. "Just as I suspected."

Now that the truth was out, she met his eyes squarely. "Papa, don't you want to hear about Nettie?" She could no longer hold back. He had to be told.

Wilhelm had turned to go up the stairs, but now his foot halted on the bottom step. "Who?" He spoke as though from a great distance, then continued on up the stairs.

"Nettie is very homesick and weak, Papa," Elise said to his back. "She wants to come home. Her first thought was for you." She almost screamed when she heard his door close. She collapsed on the bottom step and sobbed, "I didn't write letters, Papa. You told me not to correspond with her, and I didn't. I obeyed you. But I went to see her. Now what are you going to do about it?" Loudly and uncontrollably, she wept for Nettie and her father. She wept for Trevor and for herself.

❧

In the middle of the night, her door was pushed rudely open. She woke from her fitful sleep to find Justin towering over her. The moonlight streaming in the window gave light to his tall form and half of his face.

"Justin!" She sat up, startled by the intrusion.

He held a finger to his lips and whispered, "Don't be afraid, Elise. I didn't come to harm you. No one will tell me, but I know you have seen Nettie. Please tell me about her," he begged.

She heard the anguish in his voice and she hurried past him to light a small lamp. Beads of perspiration stood out on his forehead. She put a hand on his shoulder. "I saw her for only a few minutes, Justin. She is very weak and pale, but I think my visit may have helped. She was resting more easily when I left."

"But she's always been so healthy," he argued.

"Yes, and Aunt Marguerite believes she will be all right again. When the time is right, we will approach Papa again. We must wait until Nettie is recovered. I think she will be all right now. She knows we care about her."

"I thank you, Elise. You can't imagine how dreadful it is to be excluded from everything, as though I am an out-cast." He turned to go, but she heard him add thoughtfully as he went through the door, "But perhaps that is what I am—an outcast."

Elise was relieved to be alone again. As she lay back in bed, visions from her childhood crowded her sleepless night. She and Nettie had fought over a puppy, she remembered. Their mother, like always, had interceded, making peace from their arguments, reading from the big Bible.

Elise's thoughts turned to God, and she found herself asking Him once more for direction. She fell asleep at last, wondering if everyone lost their way as much as she did.

⁂

The days that followed dragged for Elise. Nothing had re-ally changed. Her father refused to talk about her visit with Nettie, and Justin moped around the house in the few minutes he was home; Inger stayed in her room and re-fused to come downstairs.

One day, Elise sat on the back stairs as she had often done as a child when she and Nettie played the listening game to discover the secrets the grown-ups hid from them. There were heat ducts connecting each room to a set of chimneys. Each duct had its own cover on the servants' back steps. The sounds from the chimney, when opened, had been like listening at the keyhole. The children had earned points for finding out the juiciest bits of gossip.

On impulse, Elise lifted the cover to her father's heat duct. She heard Inger cough loudly, and Elise jumped, looking around for anyone who might be watching her eavesdrop. She was about to replace the plate over the hole when another voice came through the duct.

"You are wrong, *Mutte*. She will marry me. We have become so close I know once she comes home she will have no other man." Elise recognized Justin's voice.

"Then why was she in such a hurry to leave here?" Inger swished as she walked about the room.

Elise clapped a hand over her mouth and her eyes grew round. They were speaking about Nettie. Her face paled under her fingers.

Inger must have been pacing the floor, for her words grew loud and faded with regularity. "Are you *verruckt*? If Wilhelm ever guessed your feelings, he would banish you from this house forever."

"But you were my mother before you became his dutiful wife," Justin laughed. "I know you will not tell him."

"You will destroy us both. If you think him to be a man of reason, you are wrong. Every day since Nettie left he threatens to send me back to Germany." She coughed violently. "You will destroy everything. You stupid idiot. Now you have a name and a place in life. If you continue with this nonsense you will have nothing. I will have nothing."

Elise stood up abruptly and replaced the vent cover with shaking hands. By yielding to a childish habit, she had already heard more than she wanted. Inger was right. Her Papa would never permit a marriage between his stepson and Nettie. No matter what Nettie had done, he would arrange a perfect match for her. Eventually, Elise knew, he would let her come home.

Justin had sounded so pitiful as he begged his mother to understand. Elise regretted now having confided Nettie's plight to him.

Her thoughts turned to Trevor. She could no longer deny her love for him, since it had been growing all her life. He had always been there, helping her through her stormy childhood, giving her strength when she needed it, reminding her of her Christian heritage. She would love him forever, she knew, but she was certain he did not return her feelings. Life seemed so hopeless, a long, narrow road leading into darkness.

At last her desperation gave way to calm and she talked to God. She promised to watch and wait. She half-chuckled at herself for making God yet another promise. But she knew He would help her grow strong enough to keep her promises.

thirteen

Nettie's return was unannounced. A Sears and Roebuck automobile piled high with boxes left her on the porch and then quickly departed. She entered the house with the air of graciousness that had always been hers, the scent of perfume floating behind her on the air. Only her stream of chatter and high-pitched laughter gave hint of her nervousness over the homecoming.

The servants fussed over her, all the while glancing over their shoulders, not knowing if they should show her to the parlor or act like she wasn't there. The sound of Wilhelm's footsteps on the stairs sent them scurrying to rooms where they could hear but not be seen, for his footsteps were as controlled as the restraint on his face. The explosion was held back, but it was coming, and each of them pitied Miss Annette.

At that moment, Elise ran down the stairs, past her father. She greeted Nettie warmly, hugging her until her sister squealed with delight, then suddenly broke into hysterical tears.

When her weeping had subsided to a few choking sobs, Nettie took her hands from her face and stared up at her father. In spite of her look of frailty, she had a new maturity and dignity about her. No one uttered a sound. Eventually a calm settled over her, and she squared her shoulders.

"You know, of course, that you are not welcome here,"

Wilhelm said, looking down through his spectacles.

"Aunt Marguerite has closed her house and gone to Europe for the spring. I can no longer stay there," she answered simply.

"What do you expect me to do, Annette?" He had not moved from his spot on the stairs.

"I wondered. . .I hoped," she stammered, "that I might stay here until I make some other arrangements. I had hoped you would finance me in a millinery shop. . .until I could repay you, of course. I want no charity," she said firmly. Having said that, she got on her knees with her head bent and her arms outstretched. "I am truly sorry, Papa. I know now that I have always been a difficult, willful child. May God forgive me. I ask that you forgive me also." Tears streamed down her cheeks. "It was unthinkable that I ran away and caused you such torment. I am sorry."

Wilhelm remained stiff and stern, but a glint in his eye gleamed where it had not been a moment ago. He came off the step and took Nettie's outstretched hands and raised her chin to look at him. Finally, he drew her close. "My Nettie, my Nettie," he whispered and bent his head to kiss her hair, completely unaware he had called her Nettie instead of Annette.

When he let her go at last, he loudly blew his nose and began barking orders to the servants who appeared in every doorway. Within a few moments, Nettie had been assigned to a suite of rooms that hadn't been opened since Edwynna's death.

The front door was flung open, and Derrick stared at Nettie. "I had no idea you were home until I saw the boxes on the porch. It's so good to see you again, Miss Annette. I came to make some wedding plans with your sister." He nodded to Elise and her father, but his attention quickly returned to Nettie's smiling face. "It is so wonderful to see you," he repeated.

The young woman who had waited so uncertainly in the vestibule only moments ago was totally in control of herself now. She was poised and gracious. She held out her hand, "How good to see you again, Derrick." She met his gaze with fluttering lashes.

Elise felt a stab of deja vu as she recognized Nettie's attentiveness. Quickly, she said, "Tell him of your plans to open a shop."

"There's time enough for all of that, dear Elise." Nettie took her father's arm and led them into the parlor. Obviously, she was home to stay—and on her own terms.

&

Nettie's homecoming was a mixed blessing. It cemented her relationship with her father but somehow alienated her from Inger and Elise. The servants doted on her wishes, often ignoring Elise, who had been managing the mansion during Inger's prolonged illness. Wilhelm's concern for his daughter extended to calling in a dressmaker to fashion a complete wardrobe for a new, slimmer Annette. His delight spread to his factory as his attention turned to the merger which would soon take his company out of the doldrums.

If Wilhelm had fallen into a new sense of peace, Inger's anxiety reached a new fervid pitch. Her son and Nettie often rode off together, staying out for hours and laughing and whispering secretively when they returned home. Inger wrung her hands and pressed her fingers to her temples, sighing with each breath.

A dramatic change had come over her son. He openly

courted Nettie with no regard for impropriety. Panic filled Inger's eyes.

ஃ

Spring broke forth around the Traum. The grounds were magnificent with the hues of azaleas and bridal wreath. In the distance, the pink and white orchards soon littered the ground with tinted snow and the promise of abundant summer fruit.

One especially crystal morning, Nettie and Justin took their ride, setting off from the stables with steam fuming from the horses' nostrils. Theirs was a leisurely ride that took them along the river and brought them back in late afternoon after a stop for a picnic lunch along the stream.

Instead of returning to the stables, Justin led the horses into the lane behind his house. Nettie humored him by following along without comment. When he gestured grandly to his house, her laughter cut through the clear air to where Inger stood on the side porch of the Traum, watching the riders dismount in the distance.

Justin helped her down, pausing a moment to stare at her golden hair and the high color that had blossomed in her cheeks since she had come home. She smiled up at him and ran to the house ahead of him, laughing all the way. He caught up with her inside and kissed her full on the lips. "Do you know how long I've been wanting to do that?"

"Justin," she reprimanded, "a brother doesn't kiss his sister like that." She walked ahead of him into the empty rooms. "We've ridden past your house a hundred times. Why is it so important to stop here today?"

"Humor me a bit longer. The house is nearly completed but it needs a woman's touch. I've had swatches of fabric and samples of wallpaper delivered. Come, see." He took her hand and led her down the hall.

"Your future wife should do that, silly."

"I want you to see everything." They entered a small solarium where late afternoon sunlight filtered from an overhead skylight through a large potted palm. A love seat graced the small area, and on a cherry table a silver tea service gleamed.

"Jus, it's lovely. I had no idea you had brought furnishings in already. What made you think of such a perfect little spot in this grand house where you could sit and bask in the sun?" She ran her fingers over the top of the table, feeling the satiny wood.

"Come see the music room. You will love the view from there. In fact you gave me the idea for the landscape one day when we were riding."

"I did?" She stared out the window at the small footbridge over the brook surrounded by wildflowers. "It's beautiful," she gasped.

"I distinctly remember you saying it would be a shame to spoil the flowers."

"Any woman would feel like a queen in this setting." She noticed the piano at one end of the room and ran her fingers over the white keys. "You have thought of everything."

He came to stand in front of her. "The house is yours, Nettie. It is you who will be my queen, dear Nettie."

Her mouth dropped open in astonishment.

He drew a fringed shawl over the grand piano and placed her picture and an oil lamp on the center.

Nettie's face registered alarm. She was seeing Justin in a new light, but what she saw was all wrong. He was her brother.

Justin's hands flew in animation. He seemed filled with such excitement, he was about to burst. "My mother knows my intentions," he boasted.

"Papa will kill you," she said flatly.

"He has already forgiven you and I shall be safe at your side." His face was filled with triumph. "I am not related to you, dear Nettie. We are related only through the marriage of our parents. From the first moment you came home from school, I knew we were meant for each other." He reached for her arm, but she pulled away.

He turned to light the oil lamp, and taking advantage of his diverted attention, she ran out of the house. She threw herself on her horse and sped to the Traum. When she dared to look back, Justin was standing by the door, his arms outstretched toward her.

She passed Elise as she hurried to her room. Surely her sister had seen the fear in her eyes, some of the repulsion she felt. But she could not tell Elise what had happened. Instead, Nettie sank to the floor of her room, pondering what to do. To tell or be silent, to ruin all their lives, or to keep the peace that now existed? This was her dilemma.

❧

Justin sat on the floor in the darkened house, moonlight streaming through the windows just as he had always imagined it. Another time he might have found the setting romantic. But he was alone. His thoughts, however confused, always returned to Nettie. He envisioned her singing in her beautiful soprano at the grand piano.

He rose to look at her picture. The moonlight gave it a cool nebulous light. He lit the lamp again and pulled on the shawl to bring her likeness closer to him. He was clumsy, and the lamp tipped, spilling the oil across the shawl.

The flames spread across the top of the piano and then into its depths. Justin lunged to contain the fire. Instead, he merely succeeded in fanning the flames with the tintype of his beloved Nettie. The picture melted in his hand and singed his fingers. He laughed bitterly. It was gone like Nettie.

He looked around him, unconcerned for his safety. Nothing was in the empty house that would burn, no draperies, no chairs or carpets, only the boxes of samples. As he looked at them, the rolls of wallpaper caught fire. The material smoldered for a few seconds before it, too, burst into flames.

From there the fire darted across the newly varnished floor to a closet where the workmen stored their supplies. When the heat reached the door, it had gained such intensity it ignited the contents with an explosion that threw Justin across the room. The weakened piano leg collapsed, and the large instrument pinned Justin to the floor.

In a matter of minutes, fire consumed the fresh timbers of the house, gutting it entirely, leaving only the marble floor at the entrance. When the intense heat and fire abated, Justin's body was found among the embers.

ஆ

For days afterward the smell of smoke hung over the valley. Justin Mueller's untimely death became linked to gossip that he had been a strange young man who never worked other than as a gardener, drifting aimlessly about the countryside like a vagrant.

Wilhelm berated himself for not paying more attention to his stepson. He became obsessed with the memory of the spilled wine, the prophecy of bloodshed. In the days that followed, he and Inger avoided contact with each other.

In her grief, Inger felt compelled to secrecy. She had

heard nothing from Nettie to indicate that Justin had revealed his secret. She lived with the realization that once her son had begun to covet Wilhelm's daughter, they were doomed. Justin's own stupidity had led him to the grave, she reasoned. Slowly, she began to put her life together, not taking any part of the blame for her son's tragic end.

Elise, however, shared her secret, though Inger never guessed it. Whatever her father's reason for keeping Inger at a distance, Elise missed the role her stepmother had played in her life. Elise would have liked to have shared their pain over Justin's death, but she kept silent. She had seen Nettie's face on the evening Justin died and fully understood that Nettie knew the truth also. Elise's heart went out to her also.

During this time of sorrow, Wilhelm rarely associated with the family. He took all his meals in his room. When he came downstairs for some business papers, he looked old and gaunt, his body racked with coughing. His gait was little more than a shuffle.

"Papa, please come to dinner," Elise implored. "We miss you. There is no one to talk to. We need you, Papa." Elise was bone weary of eating alone or with a silent Nettie, but Wilhelm would only mumble a few words and return to his room. Elise fell to her knees every night and prayed for her disintegrating family.

fourteen

When the automobile stopped on the driveway, Elise expected to soon see Derrick at the door with his usual Sunday bouquet of flowers. Instead, he was followed into the house by his father and cousin. He nodded curtly to her as they went directly to her father's library. In a few moments the Homes men were joined by Wilhelm, wearing a smoking jacket and a yellowed scarf tied loosely around his wrinkled throat.

He had been assisted from his sick bed by his faithful manservant, but on the way to the library he had coughed and wheezed and growled at the servants, all the while refusing to see a doctor. As he had passed Elise, his face was a grim mask.

Nettie stood nearby. When the door had closed behind them, she asked, "What do you think this means, Lise?" A worried frown creased her smooth brow. "I've never seen Derrick look so serious. Father's not well enough to be called from his bed at a moment's notice." Since Justin's death, she had come to call Wilhelm "Father" instead of "Papa" without even noticing it herself.

"Unless I'm mistaken," Elise answered, "it was Papa who called this meeting. He summoned a servant during the night and immediately a rider went out." She sighed and went into the parlor where she lit a small lamp to dispel the gloom that had settled over the house. "Perhaps Papa is having second thoughts about the merger."

"Father rarely has second thoughts about anything," Nettie said with half a smile, glad he had at least had second thoughts about rejecting her. She began to pace back and forth across the room.

"What's the matter, Nettie? Since you've been home you are like a caged animal. I'm the one who should be upset and anxious, not you."

Nettie shot back, "You can have it all, Lise, but you don't want the things any normal woman would want."

"Derrick is no prize, Nettie, if that's what you mean. I don't love him. I have always believed marriage should be based on love between two people. You know how I feel about the whole arrangement." They had argued frequently, always about the same subject.

Nettie's lips closed in a hard tight line as she turned away.

The front door knocker sounded, and in a few minutes a maid brought a note on a small silver tray. Elise read it silently.

"Now what's the matter?" Nettie snapped, watching her sister's expression.

"Dr. Neavitt finally left Schiffley for his daughter's home in Virginia. So many are sick right now in the town, and he collapsed under the strain of caring for so many patients. I never thought he would leave but I know he's getting older. It would be selfish to expect him to stay. I had begged him to look in on Papa before he left, but I guess he was unable to. He writes his apologies."

"I had hoped he would wait. . ."

"For Papa to die? Is that what you thought?" Elise laughed in a tight little trill that sounded across the empty room. "Why the poor man is much older than Papa. Please, give him some credit for all the years of service and dedication. He's given so much in his lifetime."

"But what will we do with both Father and Inger sick? You know they will have no other doctor." Nettie's face registered a trace of panic.

"They no longer have a choice. We will send for Trevor. There is nothing else we can do." Elise's words were simply put, but at the same time she sucked in her breath.

"Father won't like it," Nettie warned.

And what of you? Elise thought, biting back the impulse to confront her sister about Trevor. Instead, she slipped her arm about her sister's waist. "I know we have had our differences, Nettie, but we must put them aside. These are going to be difficult times for us all."

"I know you are right, Lise. There is too much between us that is good to have discord."

The library door opened and the Homes men came out. Randall Homes' jaw sagged, and his face reflected strain. Derrick's mouth was grim as he met Elise's questioning eyes. For a moment he looked at Nettie and seemed about to speak, but he hurried past Wilhelm, who was braced in the doorway, and out to the waiting automobile.

Without waiting for anyone's help, Wilhelm grasped the newel post and hoisted himself up the first step. He let out a groan and began coughing violently. Elise saw him crumble and ran to his side, but the weight of his body slid from her arms, and he collapsed in a heap on the floor. His manservant and a maid came running to help.

Nettie flew to the stable for a man to bring the doctor, while Elise helped carry Wilhelm to his room. Elise sat for a long time on the balcony, waiting for Trevor, while Wilhelm slept a deep unnatural sleep broken only by the rattling in his chest. Her mind clouded with the thought of seeing Trevor again, but her father's illness took precedent over her own feelings.

She was startled by Trevor's appearance as he came up the stairs. He was haggard and unshaven, and his strong shoulders sagged as though the weight of the world had been placed upon them. As an afterthought, Elise glanced over the railing to see if Nettie waited below. The hall was empty.

After he had made his rounds of the sick rooms, Trevor led her into the hall. "Your father is a very sick man, Elise. Inger is younger, stronger. They have both been seized by influenza. So has much of Schiffley. There are people in the churches and schools, everywhere a hospital could be set up. The epidemic shows no signs of abating. Please have as little contact as possible with them for your own protection." He placed his hand on her arm, and she felt all qualms of seeing him again vanish.

"I will do what I can to avoid catching the influenza," she promised him, "but there is no one else to look after them. Many of our servants are sick, too."

"Your father's condition is the gravest. He has double pneumonia, I fear. Keep him as comfortable as possible. All we can do is wait. I'm sorry I can offer you no help. I can't even spare my nurse, my niece Ardith."

Elise's head swam. In spite of the gravity of the situation, she felt relief: The young woman she had seen him with that day so long ago was not his sweetheart after all but a niece. Immediately, she dismissed the thought and harsh reality returned. "Are you saying my father may not survive?"

"I want you to make a tent out of linen with some hot water inside. Steam may help loosen some of the fluid in his lungs. There is little else we can do, I'm afraid." He looked deeply into her eyes. "I wish I could give you more hope, but I can't." He added bitterly, "Too bad the needs of this town couldn't have included an infirmary instead of a railroad depot."

"A depot to bring the railroad will bring prosperity to Schiffley," she defended her father's position without knowing why.

He ignored the remark with a look of disgust. "I can't stay. I am needed elsewhere. Send for me if your father's condition takes a dramatic change."

"Of course," she said, trying not to think what that change could be. She followed him to the door and found Nettie huddled in a dark corner of the parlor. She was sobbing hysterically.

"He's going to die, Lise. I just know it. Maybe I can get Trevor back." She started to the foyer, and Elise did nothing to hold her back. The outer door had closed with finality, however, and Nettie returned alone.

"Nettie, we will do all we possibly can. More than that, man or God couldn't expect of us. If it is His will, then it is Papa's time. You know what Mamma taught us, that no one knows the time or day when God will call us home. Trevor told me the whole town is caught up in this sickness. I'm tempted to offer to help where I am needed and leave you to look after Papa and Inger, but even the servants have gone home to be with their families. I don't think you could manage here alone."

"Don't ask it of me, Lise." She shook her head vehemently. "I can't do it. I hate being with the sick. But I can help you with the food and washing. You know how Mamma insisted we be taught to do everything in the house.

I can do that, Lise," she begged.

"Of course, Nettie. Whatever you can do will be appreciated. There is nothing that won't make my task easier." Elise thanked God for Nettie's offer and hoped it would be enough.

"How do you do it, Lise? You have the strength for everyone. Mamma had it too. I have heard stories about how she nursed the ones no else would." She stood by the door. "When all this is over I must tell you what I have told no one else. God keep you safe. I'm sorry, Lise. So sorry."

As Elise pondered Nettie's words, she entered her father's room and heard his cries of delirium. Her mind reeled with the tasks ahead of her. Taking to heart Trevor's words of caution to stay away from the sickness, she dragged a small mattress from the attic and laid it on the balcony between the two rooms. The few precious minutes she had between sick calls, she collapsed on the mattress and tried to rest. Through her mind's tired haze, Nettie's untold secret nagged at her.

&

"You look awful, Lise," Nettie commented several days later as she brought a bowl of oatmeal for Elise's supper. Though Nettie had learned a few skills in the kitchen, her menu was limited to gruel and soup and biscuits.

Their days were long and their nights unending. They hung damp sheets on the railings of the balcony; as soon as the sheets dried, the sisters dragged them down and carried them to be used in the sick rooms. Nettie's untidy appearance and sunken cheeks were little better than her sister's.

Elise detained her at the top of the stairs. "I fear Papa is dying, Nettie. If you have anything to tell me, I need to hear it now. It will make it easier to bear whatever the next few days has in store for us if we have no secrets."

Nettie had never seen Elise look so grim. Her voice was stern and her thin body appeared stiff, as though she willed herself to remain upright. In her face was a look of determination.

"I had hoped we could sit down and talk over a cup of tea." Nettie met her sister's unflinching gaze, recognizing that there was no postponing the inevitable.

"Papa wants a wedding," Elise said. "He hasn't said it, but I'm sure this was the reason for the meeting with Derrick and his father."

Nettie was silent and pale.

"Before I take the vows, I must ask you to share your secret with me. I am aware that Trevor took you to Aunt Marguerite's home. What is it you have to tell me, Nettie?" Elise crossed her arms on her chest and stood waiting. She swayed slightly but compensated by moving her feet ever so slightly. The large clock chimed downstairs as they faced each other.

"I thought a few days ago it would be easy to tell you." Nettie's heart thumped within her chest. "But I can't say the words." She took a deep breath. "I know you're a noble woman, Lise, much more worthy of anything good than I. I feel that I have failed you as a sister. God is punishing me. I hope you can find it in your heart to forgive me."

Elise took her hand. "Nettie, I love you. There is nothing to forgive. God is the all forgiving One, much greater than anyone knows. Before I become a married woman, I want there to be no secrets between us. Only then will I be relieved of a promise I made to you when we were children, a promise to look after you. Now you must tell me."

"Oh, Lise. It was love at first sight for both of us." She came and wept on Elise's shoulder. "But there is no hope for us. What will we do? We are condemned to a life of pain."

"What are you talking about?" Elise shook Nettie's shoulders.

"It's Derrick, Derrick I love. He loves me also."

Elise sank to her knees. Her fingers flew to her lips and tears streamed down her face. "But Trevor," she said at last. "He took you to Marguerite's."

"He offered to help me as a friend. I confided in him. He has taken an oath and he never will tell unless I release him." She knelt by Elise. "Trevor was called to a sick bed the night of the picnic. Derrick offered to see me home. We talked of our feelings—but he had made a pact with our father and his. He said he was compelled to do the honorable thing and adhere to his word and marry you, no matter what it did to our lives." Nettie buried her head in Elise's lap and sobbed as her sister's eyes glazed with a faraway stare.

❧

Wilhelm awoke from his deep sleep and tried to focus on Elise as she bathed his face with a cool cloth. His eyes were clear for the first time in days.

He said weakly, "In the morning I want you to marry Derrick, daughter. I have his consent that the marriage must not be delayed. Make the arrangements. Send word to Derrick. He is only waiting for the word."

"My birthday is still a month away. You promised me," she said.

"I told him a wedding would take place before I die." He began to cough again. Blood stained his nightshirt.

Elise fought back nausea. Her precious bid for time was gone. Of one thing she was sure, her father spoke not from delirium but from the first lucid moment he had had in days.

He grabbed her wrist. "Promise me, daughter. My body is not to leave this house until there is a wedding."

"Papa, there is too much to do," she protested. Seeing the panic in his eyes chilled every fiber in her body. She began to talk softly, hurrying on as she saw him relax slightly. "Papa, I cannot think of you standing before God unless you have accepted Him, wholly and truthfully. I know Mamma wanted to lead you to Jesus Christ, but you resisted. Please, think about your life and your soul. Accept Jesus and know His peace."

He looked at her strangely. "Oh, may God forgive me for my sins," he cried. "You don't know how many times I have longed for someone to lead me to Him since your mother died. I thought it was too late. She was gone and so was I. Do you think it is too late for me, Lise?" He whispered her pet name as he grasped her hand.

"No, Papa, God will take you home in His own time. Pray for His peace while I leave you to prepare for a wedding." A look of pure relief transformed her face as she walked from the room.

fifteen

Unexpectedly, Trevor stopped in to visit Wilhelm and Inger. A lessening of the influenza outbreak in Schiffley had closed some of the temporary shelters, and Trevor's workload was lightening. Though he still looked tired and gaunt, his appearance had improved slightly.

Nettie greeted him at the door. He hugged her and twirled her around before he started up the stairs toward Elise.

"You look like you've just seen a ghost," she observed as he stepped onto the landing.

"For a moment I thought I had," he admitted.

"It's amazing how much she looks like Mother but has . . ."

"So few of her qualities," he finished. "Nettie has more mettle than you give her credit for, though."

"You did love my mother."

"Sometimes I could shake you, Elise." He caught her hand as though he expected her to slap him. "I was nearly sixteen when she died. She was a wonderful woman who thought no more of me than to help me out of the fate I was destined for. I will always thank her for that. Yes, I was infatuated by her. Is that what you wanted to hear?"

She studied his fine features, his broad forehead and the boyish face that had reached its own maturity the past few weeks. She said nothing.

"I want to look in on your father and Inger before I go home. And then I want to take off my boots and collapse."

His smile stopped her heart. "Inger is better and Papa has rallied slightly, though I know he is dying." No smile touched her whitened lips.

"Ah, you are practicing medicine now," he teased.

"One doesn't have to be a physician to know the signs." She could not answer his smile. She wanted desperately to tell him she was sorry for her accusations about her mother but words of apology never come easily. Instead, she held herself stiffly against the railing.

Two servants had returned from their sick beds, and now one of them approached her with a note. "The food will be prepared in time, Miss Elise," the maid said.

"In time for what?" Trevor asked.

"In time for a wedding."

"A wedding? Now?" he almost shouted. "Surely you don't mean to go through with this charade?" A dark expression clouded his face. He took a step toward her.

Elise held up her hands defensively. "I have promised Papa there would be a wedding today. . .a death bed promise." Her voice shook.

His face went red with anger. "Don't let him do this to you, Elise. He has always controlled everything in his life. Don't let him continue to control you in his death."

She was startled by his rage. "It will be best for everyone. Then Schiffley will have its railroad for that empty depot you are worrying about." She tried to smile to placate his outburst, but the smile stiffened her parched lips.

He caught her shoulders. "Will you be able to live with a promise made to a dead man? Elise, you must think of yourself now. You deserve some happiness. Don't allow yourself to be controlled all your life."

"I have made a promise."

"So has your father. But apparently he thinks nothing of breaking his own promise. Your birthday is still weeks away."

"You remembered," she said softly. For an instant another memory brought her up sharply, something her father had said weeks ago in the library. Her tired brain almost caught the words, almost.

"You will never be happy with a man as domineering as Derrick Homes," Trevor said. "How can you even think to do this?" He looked at her steadily.

"What kind of a man could I be happy with, Trevor?" Her dark eyes met his unflinchingly.

"With a man who understands your need to serve the Lord. With a man who has loved you all his life."

She drew in breath. Her head felt light. "I must honor my father. My promise. . ."

"If you keep this promise, there will be no turning back for you. You will be rich and important, but you will never know true love." He turned away from her and clomped down the stairs two at a time, slamming the front door behind him.

With uncertainty in her step, Elise went back to her father's room to pray with him and prepare herself for a wedding.

❧

In a few hours Elise went to Nettie's rooms. Her sister was deep in thought, staring out the window across the field that separated the Traum from the charred remains of Justin's house.

"I'm sorry for the view, Nettie. You should have asked Papa if you could move to other rooms." Elise forced herself to look out at what had once been a magnificent house.

A shiver ran down her spine.

"I tried, but I think he wanted me to stay here—to hurt me," Nettie sighed. "And if he blamed me, I also blame myself a thousand times over. All the times I flirted so outrageously with Justin. No wonder he thought I was in love with him. I shall never forgive myself."

"Your flirtations were a part of your attack on life, dear Nettie. We all knew it and loved you in spite of it—and because of it, Justin most of all. Don't blame yourself. Justin bears a large part of the blame. He saw only what he wanted to see. The whole sordid mess was destined for failure long before the night he died."

Nettie nodded sadly, her eyes filled with pain.

Elise sank into a cushioned chair, exhausted. "Well, I prepared for a wedding like Papa instructed me to. Now we must decide what to wear."

"You mean you haven't shopped for a wedding dress yet? Your birthday is close at hand. The wedding would have taken place soon even if it hadn't been for this. . . circumstance."

Elise studied Nettie for a long moment. "So much has come between us, I wonder if we shall ever be friends."

"We are friends, Lise, just as we are sisters. Nothing will ever change that. There is one thing I can't bring myself to do, though, no matter how much I love you."

"What could that be?" Elise smiled.

After a long pause, Nettie answered, "I can't attend the wedding."

"I can't blame you for not wanting to." As though thinking aloud, she said, "We have always been rivals, Nettie. Did you know that? First for our mother, then for Papa. Our Nanny once told me that you got everything you wanted. It began with toys and puppies and the dolls Mamma left to us when she died. Then there was Papa's love. You took it all." Her words were soft but accusing nonetheless.

"That's not true," Nettie rose in self defense. "Papa never loved me for myself. He loved me because I look like Mamma. I saw it in his eyes. He never cared about *me*. When it came to being smart and knowing what to do, he always took your advice even though he might not have given you credit for it. I was the dumb one. I heard the servants say it more than once." Her eyes filled with tears that she wiped before they spilled down her cheeks.

Elise murmured, "I never thought of you that way." She wanted to say more, but she couldn't find the words.

"It was your fault, too," Nettie continued. "You constantly gave in to me. You insisted on giving me the lion's share when I didn't even want it. It made you feel in control, just like Papa. You pushed people to do your bidding, then you blamed them for taking over."

Elise sat dazed by the accusations. At last she spoke. "How can you think that? I have no control over my life. Look at me now." It was her turn to wipe her eyes.

A long uncomfortable silence drifted between them.

"I'm afraid Papa used us both," Elise said at last. "I'm so glad we had this talk, Nettie. I'm so sorry for my part in your unhappiness. Thank you for being honest with me. Mamma would be proud of you, you know. Even though you don't quote the Scriptures," she laughed lightly.

They embraced for a long moment. "We are both going to attend a wedding, Nettie, wearing the same lovely gowns we wore at the party. It is going to be a joyous occasion. We will need some witnesses so I will send out some requests. Derrick and the preacher will be here in an hour, so we must hurry." She dragged her protesting sister from the room.

Memory had eluded her at first, but at last she remembered the pact she and her father had made in the library that September morning when she requested help for her charities. Once again she thanked God for His infinite wisdom.

sixteen

Derrick had been waiting in the library for thirty-five minutes. The minister and the groomsman stood with him, chatting amiably at first, then in strained conversation. Finally, Derrick sank into one of the leather chairs, no longer making any pretense at small talk. The mantel clock ticked on amid the many volumes that filled the room to capacity. Derrick pulled on his mustache and tugged at the cuffs protruding an acceptable length from his coat sleeves.

He was dressed formally in a dark gray suit and lighter gray cravat. His hair had been slicked down for the occasion. Every few minutes he took a gold watch from his pocket and studied the Roman numerals. Finally, the door opened, and his bride came into the room accompanied by her sister and several other guests, among them the housekeeper and Trevor Lucas, who stood off to the side with a dour expression on his face.

Elise was thin and pale, he noticed. She was attired much more simply than seemed befitting the occasion, wearing the same rose ball gown as when she had been presented on the grand staircase in front of throngs of guests. A small white Bible was clutched in her gloved hands and a short veil completed her ensemble. Nettie wore the blue taffeta with pearls across the bodice. She had red-rimmed eyes and was obviously reluctant to attend the ceremony.

The minister gestured for everyone to take their places. Elise leaned forward and whispered something to him.

He hesitated.

The clock chimed six. Elise quickly removed her veil and, wordlessly, offered it to Nettie. Her sister stepped back in amazement, then turned to look at Derrick. Derrick's own look of amazement was quickly replaced with a dawning joy. He nodded eagerly, and Nettie took the veil and put it on her fair hair. She kissed Elise on the cheek as she took the small Bible from her sister's hand, and her eyes sparkled. Derrick handed Nettie the red rose he had intended for her sister.

Elise glanced at Trevor's stunned expression. In the same quick glance she also noticed he was wearing the same muddy boots he had on a few hours ago. She turned forward again, and at last everyone was in place. The ceremony began.

Derrick took Nettie's hand and pulled her closer to him. A look of great relief filled his face. The words intoned by the minister in a nasal monotone were meaningful but short. As they exchanged vows, Derrick and Nettie looked at each other lovingly. Elise's grim expression faded, and she smiled as she faced the minister.

Immediately after the ceremony, Derrick said "My dreams have just come true, Nettie, my love." They laughed and cried in each other's arms.

"Elise, I don't know how to thank you." Derrick wrung her hand. "Your Papa is a saint for permitting this," he laughed aloud.

"Papa doesn't know, Derrick. He knows only there is a wedding today. He has broken his word to me and I felt no obligation to keep mine to him. I distinctly remember him saying those exact words to me when he agreed to postpone the marriage until my birthday. Oh, it's totally legal for me to break the agreement. I checked with our attorney. It would be cruel to continue with our original plans as we both are in love with someone else." Elise sounded breathless.

A look of surprise and disapproval clouded Derrick's joy. "But what about our part of the agreement? My father will be furious that I have gone back on my word," he stammered and turned beet red. "What about the merger?"

"Come, we will talk to Papa while there is still time."

The wedding party and their guests mounted the stairs to Wilhelm's room and stood around his bed. Trevor went immediately to stand by Wilhelm's side. His dark eyes searched Elise's face.

She took her father's hand, and he roused from his fitful sleep. Nettie and Derrick stood together, hand in hand. "Papa," Elise said softly, "we have come to talk to you."

"Edwynna, it's been so long since you came to me. Forgive me for any harm I caused you."

"Hush, Wilhelm," Elise said with a catch in her breath. "I came to tell you that our daughter Annette has taken Derrick Homes for her husband." Her eyes clouded with grief as she looked to Trevor.

"A good marriage, it is. Nettie will be a good wife. Edwynna—" He began coughing violently. Trevor stepped forward to help him into a sitting position. "I have found Jesus, Eddy. . ." His words were lost in a bout of coughing so severe that it brought convulsions. His breath came in sharp stabs.

Nettie turned her face into her husband's shoulder as Elise ushered them from the room and returned to stand beside Trevor.

When her father had left them forever, she turned

toward Trevor and tearfully answered the question in his eyes. "My father wanted there to be a wedding before his body was taken from the Traum. It has been done." Then, alone, she walked from the room and made her way woodenly down the stairs.

&

Derrick Homes had left to explain the change of plans to his father. By the time he returned, the wedding finery was gone from the Traum, along with the red roses, the food, and anything else giving testimony to the event. Randall Homes accompanied his son into the library where Elise was seated behind her father's desk. She began, "As a favor to Papa, the reverend and the magistrate have both agreed to enter Nettie's name on the license instead of mine. In the morning they can go and register the papers at the courthouse. It will be uncontested."

"Every word of the merger contract will be null and void unless you marry before your sister, Miss Waller. I cannot abide by any of this." Homes slapped some papers against his leg.

"My father and I had an agreement to postpone the wedding until my eighteenth birthday. Since he saw fit to cancel the details we had agreed upon, my attorney finds no reason why I must abide by my end of the bargain. Mr. Homes, I find the happiness of my sister far outweighs the merger of your railroad and my father's business. I would think your son's future would be more important to you, also."

"Derrick and I love each other," Nettie sobbed.

"Love has nothing to do with this," he snapped. "It is a matter of keeping a gentleman's agreement." He looked helplessly at his son. "It was what Wilhelm and I agreed upon. Surely you can't expect me to take a dying man's comatose ramblings as an acceptance of their marriage. It didn't change the contract. He insisted his eldest daughter was to be wed first."

"I can't help it if the railroad never comes to Schiffley. And I refuse to take the blame for it. I'm so tired of playing games," Elise confessed and sank in her seat. Her voice shook. "There will be a reading of the will in a short time. Perhaps you should hold your decision until then, Mr. Homes."

Derrick came to stand beside Elise. He took her hand. "I owe you a debt I can never repay. I will reason with my father, for whatever it is worth."

"Thank you, Derrick. You are to be present for the reading, also."

When they were gone and the stillness of the house became unbearable, Elise walked outside, hardly seeing the beautiful lines of the sculptured gardens and shrubs that Justin had cultivated so lovingly. Even without the flowers, they looked clean and ordered, much as she wanted her life to be. At last she sat on the stone bench facing the small pond where tiger lilies bloomed in summer. The frosty air made her shiver, but it brought reason to her dulled senses. A voice behind her spun her around.

"The weight of the world is on those shoulders," Trevor said, smiling down at her.

"I didn't hear you coming," she explained "I want to apologize for blaming you for not telling me about Nettie. I know now you had sworn a sacred oath. I was wrong for blaming you."

"I wanted to tell you so often. I could feel your pain. It is I who am sorry, Elise."

"We have a truce then, Trevor?" She held out her hand.

"A truce for now. But someday you must tell me what it's like impersonating a maid, a pretty one, too, I might add." He took her hand and held it as she turned crimson. "I know Nettie loves Derrick and it changed the outcome of the wedding today. Who is it that you love, Elise? I have a feeling it also altered your decision to marry a man selected by your father." Trevor stood looking down at her, his eyes wide and dark, loving her with their warmth.

She blushed again. "Do I have to tell you, Trevor? Isn't it plain for all the world to see?"

"It would be wonderful to hear it from your lips," he said quietly.

"I have loved you all my life, Trevor. How could you not know?"

"I was hoping you felt that way when you returned from school—but when you became betrothed, I no longer believed it possible."

"Oh, Trevor. I was helpless in the face of my father's plans. I wanted so much to do his will, to be a dutiful daughter. I didn't know how to escape. I prayed to God to show me a way. And He did," she cried. "I never meant to defy Papa. I loved him. One of the happiest days of my life was when he accepted Jesus as his Savior. And whether he knew it or not, he gave me the way out. I can't believe he didn't know." She went into Trevor's arms and looked up at him. "Did you really love me all your life?"

"Oh, my beloved. I have loved you since you were a little girl and I urged you to go away to school. Even then, I must have realized what a wonderful, kind and caring woman you would become. I haven't been mistaken. What torture you have endured! Our lives will be so different

from this moment on. I love you with all my heart, Elise."
He kissed her and they joined hands as they walked to the
house for the reading of the will.

❧

The servants and family and a few friends were assembled
in the parlor. Elise circulated among them as they waited
for the attorney to make his appearance. Inger waited by
the desk next to Elise's empty chair. Substantially recovered from her bout of influenza, Inger shuddered at the
thought of returning to Germany, which she fully expected
to be the message Wilhelm's will would have for her. Nettie,
on her right, was tired and dejected, drained of the joy of
her wedding by the strain of the past few days. She made
no move to help Elise calm the fears of the staff. She was
as concerned about her own future as they were about theirs.

At long last, the pocket doors of the parlor opened and a
small refined-looking gentleman was ushered into the room.
He closed the door with a snap of the latch that was felt by
everyone.

Mr. Comstock made a ritual of spreading his papers
across the desk that had been brought in for that purpose.
He shuffled them a dozen times until he was sure they were
properly in order. With spectacles in hand, he called for
silence and disposed of the bequeaths to servants and housekeeper with speed. When they were dismissed, he motioned
the family closer for the private portion of the will.

Comstock droned his legal jargon. When Inger heard her
name, she stiffened, leaning ahead slightly to catch every
word. She was to be given a modest sum and had the choice
of returning to Germany or remaining at the Traum for the
rest of her life. She sobbed quietly into a handkerchief in
utter relief.

Next in order was the granting of a modest sum to Elise to continue her charities in Schiffley. She was stunned by a generous amount to begin a fund for an infirmary.

"Herewith are disclosed the following disbursements of the estate." Comstock paused and once satisfied he had everyone's undivided attention, continued. "To Derrick Homes I bequeath the sum of $500 dollars a month to manage the estate and mill. In the period of one year, if a profit has not been made in the silk mill, an attorney shall appoint a new manager. Each year a profit has been made, his salary shall be reviewed and adjusted accordingly."

Derrick brushed an imaginary fleck of lint from his coat. His expression was slightly subdued, but he brightened when he looked at Nettie.

"And now to the main portion of the will." Comstock adjusted his glasses and took a deep breath. "Though the entire estate: the Traum, all acreage, lower farm, horses and stables, silk mill, and any other properties in my name at the time of my death, are entrusted to the management of Derrick Homes, they shall remain the real property of my daughters, Elise, two-thirds share, and Annette, one-third share."

Elise's mouth fell open. Derrick was instantly on his feet, protesting loudly. Nettie simply sat, wide-eyed, a look of total confusion on her face.

Comstock stood up, but he was dwarfed by Derrick as the younger man ran around the room, his arms flailing. Softly, the old man banged on a pile of papers with his spectacles, calling for order amid chaos.

Several thoughts raced through Elise's mind as she sat dumbstruck. Had she been married to Derrick at that moment he would have shared in her inheritance, which surely was what her father had intended. Her hands shook as she wiped cold perspiration from her brow.

"You tricked me," Derrick accused, pointing his finger at Elise. "You must have known what was in your father's will when you forced me into marriage with Nettie."

Elise flinched when she saw the look of hurt that filled Nettie's eyes. "No one forced you," she reminded Derrick. "You love Nettie, remember?"

Derrick looked at his bride and shame filled his face. "Of course I love her. But—"

"Mr. Homes, please be seated so I can continue," Comstock pleaded. He picked up the will and began to read once more. "If there is any breech of contract on the part of Derrick Homes to capably look after the best interests of his wife and sister-in-law, the entire management of the estate shall fall into the capable hands of my daughter, Elise. This concludes the reading of the last will and testimony of Wilhelm Waller."

Derrick slumped in his seat, a defeated expression on his face. Immediately after the reading, he left to consult his father.

Nettie broke the silence. "I know Derrick loves me. But he was saying earlier that this is a terrible time to begin a marriage in the midst of all this upheaval. He is right. I feel so sorry for him. I want to help him but I don't know how."

"Maybe we can help him, after all." Elise patted Nettie's shoulder. "Please ask Trevor to come in. He's been waiting in the parlor. The three of us have something to discuss, but first I must do something upstairs."

Moving like a sleepwalker, she went to her father's room and sat by his empty bed. Thoughts of the past crowded the thoughts of the future. The picture of her father's village in Germany hung over his bed, reminding her of his poor beginning. But tomorrow, once she had found her way through today's troubles, she would have time for remembering her father. Right now, her world was still troubled.

She had touched on an idea that might salvage all their futures, though. She had come to accept Derrick, not as a husband, but as a brother-in-law who would look after her as a sister. If he would agree to her plan, they might all have a chance for happiness after all.

❧

When Derrick returned, he was accompanied once again by his father. "There is nothing good to come out of this whole mess, Elise. Your father has cheated us all. We will have only discord in our lives if we live by his arrangement."

"Not if we can work out our futures now, Derrick," she answered.

"What could you possibly want, Elise? You have everything. Nettie is to be practically penniless. There is no merger, nothing."

"We have a plan that would benefit us all and allow us to live in harmony. I hope you will agree to it. I want the mill to be operated to the benefit of its employees. It must be fair and decent to them, and I am to have a part in making the decisions that will create a better life for the workers. I request a separate deed for the lower farm and buildings so Trevor and I can help the homeless and orphaned. All of us are to share equally in any profit from the business. Most of all, Derrick, I want you and Nettie to have the Traum, the only stipulation being that you look after Inger. It is up to your father, Derrick, if there is still to be a merger."

"I think my father could be persuaded to those terms." He looked across the room where Randall Homes had been standing quietly on the sidelines.

"It was a silk mill I had bargained for," the older man commented, "but I got so much more, a family I never dreamed of. And I do mean all of you," he said, spreading his arms. "But there is one other matter that is not entirely satisfactory," he said gravely. "Elise, your father insisted you were to be married first or the agreement was not to be honored."

Quietly, Trevor stepped forward. "I think that can be arranged to suit all parties involved. This time we shall have a formal wedding with both sisters as brides, but Elise will take the first vows, and Nettie, the second. A double wedding would do just fine." He smiled and looked lovingly into the eyes of his future bride.

Nettie came to stand beside Elise. She hugged her tightly and whispered, "For one more time, Lise, we shall be sisters in the sun."

A Letter To Our Readers

Dear Reader:

In order that we might better contribute to your reading enjoyment, we would appreciate your taking a few minutes to respond to the following questions. When completed, please return to the following:

Rebecca Germany, Editor
Heartsong Presents
P.O. Box 719
Uhrichsville, Ohio 44683

1. Did you enjoy reading *Sisters in the Sun*?
   ❑ Very much. I would like to see more books
      by this author!
   ❑ Moderately
      I would have enjoyed it more if _____

   _____

2. Are you a member of *Heartsong Presents*? Yes   No
   If no, where did you purchase this book? _____

   _____

3. What influenced your decision to purchase this
   book? (Check those that apply.)

   ❑ Cover   ❑ Back cover copy

   ❑ Title   ❑ Friends

   ❑ Publicity   ❑ Other _____

4. On a scale from 1 (poor) to 10 (superior), please rate the following elements.

   ___Heroine   ___Plot

   ___Hero   ___Inspirational theme

   ___Setting   ___Secondary characters

5. What settings would you like to see covered in *Heartsong Presents* books?

6. What are some inspirational themes you would like to see treated in future books?_____

7. Would you be interested in reading other *Heartsong Presents* titles?   ❏ Yes   ❏ No

8. Please check your age range:
❏ Under 18   ❏ 18-24   ❏ 25-34
❏ 35-45   ❏ 46-55   ❏ Over 55

9. How many hours per week do you read? _____

Name _____

Occupation _____

Address _____

City _____ State _____ Zip _____

Don't miss these favorite Heartsong Presents *titles
by some of our most distinguished authors!*
(Voted favorites by our readers in a recent poll.)

Your price is only $2.95 each!

___HP59 EYES OF THE HEART, *Maryn Langer*
___HP62 THE WILLING HEART, *Janelle Jamison*
___HP66 AUTUMN LOVE, *Ann Bell**
___HP70 A NEW SONG, *Kathleen Yapp**
___HP76 HEARTBREAK TRAIL, *VeraLee Wiggins*
___HP78 A SIGN OF LOVE, *Veda Boyd Jones**
___HP81 BETTER THAN FRIENDS, *Sally Laity**
___HP82 SOUTHERN GENTLEMAN, *Yvonne Lehman**
___HP83 MARTHA MY OWN, *VeraLee Wiggins*
___HP84 HEART'S DESIRE, *Paige Winship Dooley*
___HP85 LAMP IN DARKNESS, *Connie Loraine**
___HP86 POCKETFUL OF LOVE, *Loree Lough**
___HP87 SIGN OF THE BOW, *Kay Cornelius*
___HP88 BEYOND TODAY, *Janelle Jamison*
___HP90 CATER TO A WHIM, *Norma Jean Lutz**
___HP92 ABRAM MY LOVE, *VeraLee Wiggins*

*contemporary title

··· Hearts ❤️ ong ····

Any 12 *Heartsong Presents* titles for only $26.95 *

HISTORICAL ROMANCE IS CHEAPER BY THE DOZEN!

Buy any assortment of twelve *Heartsong Presents* titles and save 25% off of the already discounted price of $2.95 each!

*plus $1.00 shipping and handling per order and sales tax where applicable.

HEARTSONG PRESENTS TITLES AVAILABLE NOW:

(If ordering from this page, please remember to include it with the order form.)

·········· Presents ··········

Great Inspirational Romance at a Great Price!

Heartsong Presents
Love Stories Are Rated G!

That's for godly, gratifying, and of course, great! If you love a thrilling love story, but don't appreciate the sordidness of popular paperback romances, **Heartsong Presents** is for you. In fact, **Heartsong Presents** is the *only inspirational romance book club*, the only one featuring love stories where Christian faith is the primary ingredient in a marriage relationship.

Sign up today to receive your first set of four, never before published Christian romances. Send no money now; you will receive a bill with the first shipment. You may cancel at any time without obligation, and if you aren't completely satisfied with any selection, you may return the books for an immediate refund!

Imagine. . .four new romances every month—two historical, two contemporary—with men and women like you who long to meet the one God has chosen as the love of their lives. . .all for the low price of $9.97 postpaid.

To join, simply complete the coupon below and mail to the address provided. **Heartsong Presents** romances are rated G for another reason: They'll arrive *Godspeed!*
